# Haunted
# ALASKA

## Ghost Stories from the Far North

by Ron Wendt

EPICENTER PRESS

*Alaska Book Adventures*

Epicenter Press is a regional press founded in Alaska whose interests include but are not limited to the arts, history, environment, and diverse cultures and lifestyles of the Pacific Northwest and high latitudes. We seek both the traditional and innovative in publishing nonfiction books, and contemporary art and photography gift books.

Publisher: Kent Sturgis
Cover and Book Design: Elizabeth Watson, Watson Design
Map: Marge Mueller, Gray Mouse Graphics
Proofreader: Sherrill Carlson
Index: Sherrill Carlson
Printer: CDS Publications

ISBN 0-945397-77-1

Booksellers: This title is available from major wholesalers. Retail discounts are available from our trade distributor, Graphic Arts Center Publishing Co., PO Box 10306, Portland, OR 97210. Photo 800-452-3032.

PRINTED IN CANADA

First Edition
First Printing, October 2002

10 9 8 7 6 5 4 3

To order single copies of HAUNTED ALASKA, mail $9.95 plus $3.95 for Priority Mail shipping (WA residents add an additional 85 cents state sales tax) to: Epicenter Press, PO Box 82368, Kenmore, WA 98028.

Discover exciting ALASKA BOOK ADVENTURES! Visit our online Alaska bookstore and art gallery at www.EpicenterPress.com, or call our 24-hour, toll-free hotline at 800-950-6663

# Dedication

*To my wife, Bonnie, for her love and
support and unending help.*

# Acknowledgments

I would like to express my thanks to the people
at the University of Alaska Anchorage/Matanuska-Susitna
College Library for their great help and expertise
in finding historical documents.
Also thanks to the many Alaskans who enjoyed
sharing their stories with me.

# Contents

# Preface to a Haunting

*Haunted Alaska* is a collection of stories about scary places in the Far North, places with ghosts. These ghosts appear out of nowhere, talk, play the piano, smoke their pipes, slam doors, shake beds, touch people, and much, much more.

I make the following disclaimer about the ghosts in *Haunted Alaska:* I'm not an expert on wandering spirits; I'm not a ghost buster. But I've talked to a lot of people who have crossed paths with these spectral beings. The stories in this book are about those eerie encounters, as experienced by many folks across Alaska and the Yukon.

Some people were reluctant to tell their stories; who would believe them? Others gladly related their weird personal tales. Encounters with the dead continue to haunt the haunted and are forever etched in their memories.

There are those who believe in ghosts and those who don't. In my own life, I've had my share of experiences that verge on the supernatural. But I've bumped into a ghost only once. (I'll reveal some of my personal adventures in the pages of this book.)

My travels throughout Alaska and the Yukon have taken me to abandoned towns—there's a reason we call them ghost towns—and to old cemeteries, and up nameless creeks where I've slept in dilapidated cabins dating back over a hundred years.

I have had much delight in these quiet historical places, yet I've also experienced a sense of sadness in thinking of the people who once lived there. Perhaps they passed into the other dimension reluctantly. Each gravestone stands as testament to a life. And as I've wandered through the past, among tombstones and along the streets of once-thriving communities, I often feel someone is watching me. This curious feeling has led me to seek out the stories of those who have known firsthand the sheer surprise, or terror, of seeing a specter.

My grandfather once told me that Grandma appeared at the foot of his bed for a couple of weeks after her death. Grandpa finally explained to her that she didn't belong there anymore, that her life was over. She never appeared again.

Apparently no one is exempt from meeting a spook. The religious and the nonreligious alike tell tales of ghosts they have known. In talking with people about their spectral connections, I found no agreement on the question of why spirits roam the earth, or why ghosts manifest themselves to us.

The people willing to talk about their encounters tell me that ghostly activity in a home or a hotel seems to occur when changes are afoot—when the residents are remodeling the building, moving furniture, hosting a lot of visitors, or otherwise causing a commotion. Apparently this is unsettling for ghosts, who then make their presence known.

The good news is that, in most cases, these apparitions have proved harmless.

This book reveals many strange hauntings, of one sort or another. But the connecting message they bring is that we are not alone. There are dimensions and principalities beyond those we can see, with mysteries that baffle, amaze, and terrify. So sit back and relax, if you can, and read about the ghosts that lurk in *Haunted Alaska*.

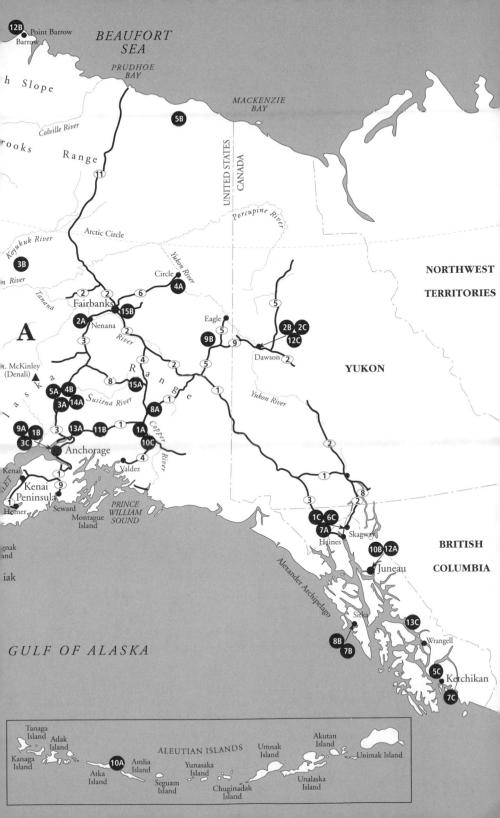

# CAUTION:

Don't read this book
before you go to bed,
or
when you are alone on
a dark, stormy night.

ONE MORNING THE GHOST CAME IN,

SAT ON THE BED, AND TOOK MY ALARM CLOCK

AND THREW IT ACROSS THE ROOM.

# No Time to Mess with a Ghost

IT WAS ON A CHRISTMAS EVE in the late 1930s, in the lobby of the Copper Center Lodge. Squeaky Pete was talking, telling stories of the old days and looking for company during the holidays.

Squeaky kept talking and talking to Don Green, who was sitting on a couch. But Green wasn't answering.

"Aren't you listening to me, Donny?" Squeaky asked.

About that time, Art Laverty came through. Laverty had attended Oxford University in England, where he had been a classmate of Winston Churchill. He was also the designer of the famous Kuskalana Bridge along the Copper River & Northwestern Railroad heading to

McCarthy, a great feat of engineering. Now Laverty was the maintenance man at the lodge. A modest man, Laverty liked to say his greatest engineering feat was building an archway into the dining room at the lodge, which he had redesigned so that it looked like an English country house.

As Art came into the lobby, Squeaky Pete called out: "Art, what's the matter with Donny Green? He's not answering me."

Art went over to Green, then told Squeaky: "He's not answering you because he's dead. You probably bored him to death."

They figured Green had been dead for about half an hour. Since it was winter and the ground was still frozen, they couldn't bury him. So they hauled the body out to the old washhouse behind the lodge. Then they went ahead with the Christmas Eve party.

Could Donny Green be haunting the Copper Center Lodge?

Rumors are plentiful. There are those who believe the lodge is haunted and those who don't. Jean Ashby Huddleston, a retired speech teacher for the University of Alaska, is convinced it is—and she suspects the haunting is by Donny Green. She has experienced it over and over again through the years.

Jean's parents, George and Katherine Ashby, bought the Copper Center Lodge in 1948, when Jean was ten years old. It wasn't long before she discovered it was haunted.

"It was spooky to go up in the attic in the middle of the night when it was dark," Jean said. "For that matter, it was spooky anytime."

The lodge was established in July 1898 by Andrew Holman on a site at the confluence of the Klutina and Copper Rivers, as a roadhouse to provide shelter for gold prospectors. He set up a couple of tents, calling one of them Hotel Holman. He soon built a trading post and a substantial log hotel to replace the tent.

The business passed through many hands before it finally became the home of Jean Ashby Huddleston and the ghost. Ringwald Blix

took over the Hotel Holman in 1906, then sold it in 1918 to Hans
Ditman, who sold it five years later to the local postmaster, Florence
"Ma" Barnes. The front half of the roadhouse was destroyed by fire
in 1932. The new two-story log roadhouse that was then built on
the site was named the Copper Center Lodge and Trading Post.

Then it was the turn of the Ashbys and their daughter Jean.

"There were things that happened," she said, "not only to me but
to other people. We never really told our ghost stories because mother
didn't believe in it, so we just kind of brushed it under the rug.

"I was in bed one night and someone came in and sat on the bed.
There's that feeling where the edge of the bed sinks down. . . . Then
there's the feeling of uneasiness. I just kind of moved over to my side
of the bed to get away from it.

"This is no time to mess with a ghost," she said with a laugh.
"I looked over and there was nobody there."

Was Donny Green the nighttime visitor? Jean thinks so, but
others believe it could have been the spirit of a man named Fox, a
journalist from the East Coast who was at the lodge back when Ma
Barnes ran the place. He was a boyfriend of Ma Barnes, and an
antagonistic fellow. Fox died at the lodge.

Jean had other visits from the phantom lodger.

"One morning the ghost came in again," she said, "and sat on
the bed and took my alarm clock and threw it across the room."

She tells of lying in bed at night and hearing footsteps going down
the hall. Not so unusual in a hotel, you might think. But, "when
you're the only one in the lodge and you hear this, it's a little spooky."

The ghostly visits took an odd turn one night.

"I had a lot of dyspepsia and I'd occasionally belch out loud in the
lobby when I was by myself at night. I stepped outside my bedroom
door one day and someone belched right in my ear!

"I thought, *oh alright, I got the message!*"

Jean moved away from the lodge for a time, but returned to

Copper Center to help her mother run the business after her father died in 1979. The ghost—whether Donny Green or the journalist Fox—was still making the rounds.

The rooms at the Copper Center Lodge are very quiet and make every traveler feel comfortable, usually.

"Some fellow who stayed there recently told me about this ghost coming in and sitting on his bed," Jean said.

George Ashby did some remodeling to the lodge during his years there, such as turning the old store into a guest room. It was a change that may have upset the ghost. The story told most often by lodge guests is of an apparition sitting on the bed. It usually happens in room 3D—the old store.

Jean Huddleston relates another unsettling incident:

"One of my grandkids refused to go down the hall into the wing.

"Her mother said 'Why?'

"She said: 'Because I'm scared of that man that's always standing there.'"

## Knik: Voices in the Woods

A FEW OF THE OLD-TIMERS of Knik say you can still hear voices of the departed, calling from the woods or from Knik Lake. On a late spring or summer evening, you can walk through the stands of birch and spruce trees near this old gold-rush town in Southcentral Alaska and imagine these sounds. In the woods are hidden reminders of the culture that once thrived here.

It was in Knik that George Purches, a local resident, got in a shootout over a woman. Purches didn't survive. The pool hall where he was killed in 1909 still stands in Knik, but it now serves as the Knik Museum. Out behind the museum is a small Indian cemetery, with graves that are maintained by local Natives.

Bands of Denaina Indians often came to Knik from nearby camps and villages. Some say that a little Indian girl drowned many years ago in Knik Lake. After that, at certain times, a small voice could be heard crying out for help from the middle of the lake.

Near Knik in the 1920s, Indian children would play in the woods off the main wagon trail out of town. During the spring, some children would hear voices coming from an ancient hunting camp nearby. They could smell smoke, hear dogs barking, and hear the hunters talking, laughing, and shouting. When the children would go to look, they would find no one.

On a late evening in these woods, many still feel the presence of a bygone era.

## Tale End: An Eternal Vigil

*The Golden North Hotel in Skagway is said to be Alaska's oldest operating hotel.*

*It's also very haunted. Many accounts of a specter seen in room 24 have been told through the years. The ghost's name is Mary, and hers is a sad story.*

*As old-timers tell it, Mary was waiting at the hotel for her fiancé to return from the Yukon goldfields when he was killed in the famous April 3, 1898, snowslide at Chilkoot Pass.*

*The despondent Mary refused to believe he was dead and would not leave her room. She eventually died of tuberculosis.*

*There is another version of Mary's story. In this one, she had been married earlier in the day and was waiting up in the room for her new husband for their wedding night. He never arrived. He had been killed in a card game downstairs. In despair, Mary jumped to her death from the window of the room.*

*Mary is now seen most often in room 24, where she continues to wait for the return of her man.*

15

RICK AWOKE TO THE SENSATION OF BEING
TIPPED OUT OF BED. HE BEGAN TO UNDERSTAND
THAT HE WAS NOT ALONE IN THE ROOM.

# A Restless Night in Nenana

FIFTY-EIGHT MILES south of the Alaska Interior city of Fairbanks lies
the small Tanana River town of Nenana. The experiences of many
folks in Nenana through the years have left them with fond memories.
But some memories aren't so pleasant.

Nenana plays a strategic role in river transportation up and down
the Tanana and Yukon Rivers. The railroad brings supplies to this
point, which are then carried by boat to dozens of river communities.
President Warren G. Harding was here in 1923 to drive the golden
spike at the north end of the bridge connecting the Alaska Railroad
from Seward to Fairbanks, completing construction of the line.

Railroad worker Rick Rapuzzi has one memory that is etched in his mind, of an experience he would just as soon forget.

Rick was working as a brakeman on a snow removal train in February 1990. He and his fellow workers were heading south from Fairbanks, removing snow from the railroad route. The crew had been putting in twelve- and fourteen-hour days as storms loaded the tracks with fresh snow.

The crew had planned to stop at the Healy station for the night, but they made it only as far as Nenana. The railroad had arranged lodging for the workers. They were directed to the Corner Hotel Bar & Grill on the town's main street, within walking distance of the station, where several guest rooms were waiting.

Street lamps and the lights of homes and businesses cast shadows and reflections on the deeply piled snow as the tired workers made their way down the street. The cold days and hard labor had exhausted them, and they were ready for a good night's rest.

"We were let into the Corner Bar and assigned rooms," Rick said. "I believe mine was number 5. After stowing our gear, we all hurried to a cafe up the street who had agreed to stay open just for us. After a hot meal we all retired back to our rooms."

The rooms in the old building were clean, but well worn, with a shared bathroom down the hall.

"I decided on leaving the door to my room unlocked and slightly ajar so I might make a quick exit in case of fire," Rick said.

"I was just drifting off to sleep when I heard a whistling, wailing noise and looked up to see the gauzy, light curtains from the window at the head of my bed stand straight out into the room. I got up to investigate, thinking the window might be partly open.

"After checking the window, I discovered it to be a kind that did not open. Also, there was plastic over the window to keep out the cold. I checked for drafts around it and found none. I looked outside onto Main Street and it was dead calm, no wind at all."

Rick went back to sleep. But two hours later, he awoke to the sensation of being tipped out of bed.

"It was as if the bed were tilted in a way that would spill me on to the floor. I was still half asleep but began to understand that I was not alone in that room. I got the feeling of a presence there.

"I don't know why, but I felt this presence to be that of an older Native man. He seemed angry and unhappy that I was there in his bed and room. I was not scared, but more annoyed than anything else. This entity seemed not to want to hurt me, but just wanted me out. I tried to ignore it and went back to sleep."

About two more hours, Rick awoke again to the feeling that he was being lifted or levitated off the bed. He looked down at his lower body and saw what seemed to be an orange glow or aura with blue sparks in it surrounding his legs. But still Rick stayed in the room, despite the unnerving presence that confronted him.

"I guess it finally gave up, because I was not bothered the rest of the night."

In the morning, he even said goodbye to the ghost.

"I turned and told the entity that I was leaving, I was sorry I had disturbed it and that I would not be back.

"I swear this all to be true and have never experienced anything like it again."

## The Ladue House: Footsteps on the Stairs

AFTER STUART AND NANCY SCHMIDT bought the old Ladue house in Dawson, in Canada's Yukon Territory, in 1997, things started happening. Lights went on and off by themselves; the sound of footsteps came from unoccupied rooms.

Joe Ladue was an early Yukoner, one of the first gold prospectors into the area in the 1880s. He set up a sawmill even before the town of Dawson was born, and he milled his way to a fortune. While others were out on the creeks mining gold, Ladue was cutting down trees, milling the lumber, and building saloons and hotels. Around the turn of the century, he built a two-story house for himself in Dawson.

The house eventually was purchased by the Schmidts, who mined gold near Dawson and also operated a jewelry store in town that specialized in gold-nugget jewelry.

Nancy Schmidt recalls her experience at the Ladue house with a stereo that refused to shut up.

"I had just turned off the stereo, and we were just leaving to go to the dump. . . . I turned off the stereo, locked up the door, ran down the stairs to the street, and got in the truck.

"Stuart says, 'Nancy, you didn't turn the stereo off.'

"'Yes I did, I just turned it off.'

"So I rolled down the window. You could hear it. Sure enough the stereo's on. I came in, turned it off. I thought, well, maybe I just didn't push the right buttons. So I turned it off, looked at it, and made sure it was turned off. I locked up the door, ran downstairs, got in the truck.

"Off we went and came back a half hour later. . . . The stereo's back on again and the music is even louder. It was blasting!

"I came in and turned it off and we were all in shock!"

A friend of Nancy's stayed at the house one night when no one else was there. After she went upstairs to bed, she heard footsteps downstairs. Then the footsteps began ascending the stairs.

"When you hear the footsteps going up the stairs, they make a real distinct sound," Nancy said. "The wood creaks, and the stepping sounds are very clear on the wood stairs."

The friend called out, then went to the top of the stairs and said, "Hello, hello," trying to find out if someone was there.

Nobody answered.

Nancy says her friend "just got chills. She got complete chills up her spine. Something was there with her."

The "something" never materialized, and the friend spent a nervous night in the creaky old house.

## Tale End: A Place of Sadness

*On the upper 60 Mile River in Canada's Yukon Territory, you may still see remnants of the abandoned town of 60 Mile. The place is remote, and not many people ever try to go there. The ghost of 60 Mile would like to keep it that way.*

*An old grave sits on a hill along the river, with a cabin nearby. It is a site of much sadness and mystery, according to the stories of people who have been there in recent decades. Visitors who have stayed in the cabin or camped in the area tell of incidents that could be the work of a phantom that is angry at being disturbed.*

*They have found objects mysteriously knocked over, and report tools disappearing. Some visitors to the grave have felt overwhelmed with sadness or become physically ill. For people who have been in the presence of the ghost of 60 Mile, the message is clear: Keep out.*

ROOM 1 IS WHAT WE CALL THE
HAUNTED ROOM. MOST OF THE ACTION
COMES FROM THAT ROOM.

# 'We Got Ghosts'

HE'S BEEN SEEN roaming the upstairs hallway. He doesn't like a certain song that's played on the jukebox. But wait a minute. Is there more than one ghost that haunts the Talkeetna Fairview Inn?

There are very few paved roads in Talkeetna. For that matter, there are very few roads. Typical of small, old Alaska communities, Talkeetna is woven together with dirt roads and quaint structures. Many of the old buildings are occupied, but a few are dilapidated and abandoned. Talkeetna, along the banks of the Big Susitna River, dates back to 1914, when the town site was laid out as a community serving the Cache Creek Mining District.

There are at least a couple of ghosts in town, and they seem to like the Talkeetna Fairview. A lot of history has marched through the old inn, a landmark in downtown Talkeetna. You can't miss it as you drive down the main street. It's the place to visit when you're there.

If you talk with the regulars at the inn, they'll probably acknowledge the ghostly beings. They're even pretty sure they know who they are. The friendly spirits that haunt the inn have developed a reputation: apparently they still live the way they did when they were alive, in a partying fashion.

Rick Shields, maintenance man at the Fairview, says he knows who the ghosts are. The resident spirits are Jim Schaff and Rocky Cummins.

"We've got pictures of them on the wall here," Rick said. "Rocky was a trapper and miner and Jim Schaff was more of a gardener and worked for the military, and he hated dandelions. Jim was a nice guy; he was actually the nicest of the two. Rocky was the miner-trapper rowdy guy. In their day they liked to party."

And what do they like to do now?

"Every once in a while, we have people stay here and the toilets will start flushing by themselves or the napkins will be thrown around or somebody will lock their door on them," Rick said. "Sometimes I'll be here late by myself and you get one of those cold rushes. . . . It's like there's something watching you. You just can't quite put your finger on it."

"Sometimes the water is turned on when I get here. Things have been moved around. Jim used to knock a can of beer off the wall when everyone was sitting there; it wasn't the wind."

Visitors who stay at the inn when there are no other guests have heard footsteps and the creaking of doors.

Rick says these visitors will tell him something like: "I thought I was the only one here last night, but I could hear somebody walking around."

Rick's response to such comments: "Well, nobody was here. It was probably the ghost."

The visitor then gasps and says, "You don't mean you have ghosts."

"Oh, yeah, we got ghosts."

"Room 1 is what we call the haunted room," Rick says. "Most of the action comes from that room. Sometimes there'll be pounding sounds on the wall or the wriggling of the doorknob. It always seems to be based around room 1. That's where the boys usually stayed."

One winter, a couple was staying in a room upstairs. As the man walked down the hall to the bathroom, he saw another man standing in the hall. The first man nodded and said "Good morning" to the dark figure in the hallway before proceeding to the bathroom.

When the first man returned to his room, he commented to his wife on the figure he had seen in the hall.

"I thought you said we were the only ones up here staying in the whole inn."

"We are," his wife reassured him.

Collette Delaney recalls that when Jim Schaff was alive, he tried to avoid loud music. "We used to have an old jukebox and it was over in the corner where a slot machine sits now," she said. "He hated loud music. It was his biggest gripe in life."

In the period after Jim died, a tune called "The Rodeo Song" was often played on the jukebox.

"There's a lot of cussin' and it's pretty wild," Collette said of the song. "They used to put that on really loud, real late at night, and the jukebox would shut down. We say it was Jim shutting it down and complaining about the noise."

Another time, patrons observed what they thought might have been Jim's ghostly presence. They were celebrating his birthday, and a can of his favorite beer kept flying off the shelf and hitting the bartender on the head. Perhaps the old-timer wanted his favorite suds.

## Deadman's Camp: A Friendly Spirit

WHEN STATE TROOPERS first opened the door of the cabin at remote Deadman's Camp, a cloud of black flies emerged. Inside, they found the body of the old man.

Deadman's Camp, north of Mount Tozi in the Ray Mountains, is surrounded by streams: Torment Creek, Fleshlanana Creek, Gishna Creek, and the Tozitna and Kilolitna Rivers. The camp is also near a hidden draw called Spooky Valley.

In the 1940s, a gold miner named Mayo vanished near here. He had been known by many people and was seen numerous times just before his disappearance. Some say his ghost now wanders the valley.

The area's most intriguing tale concerns the old man who lived in the cabin at Deadman's Camp. One spring, the man failed to emerge from the cabin, says Fairbanks resident Lynette Clark.

"The troopers flew into the area because some people checked on the old-timer and found him dead," Lynette said. "There was no foul play. He was an elderly man and the bush had beat him up pretty bad, but he still enjoyed living out there."

Lynette says the cabin "never lost its sense of being lived in," even though it sat empty for years.

"There were clothes still hanging in the closet. There were shirts still in new wrappers that he'd bought from town. It was almost like you could walk in and have dinner with this old guy."

Whoever he was, he had been there a long time and appeared to have had a happy life at the cabin. He obviously took pride in his home, with wood detailing and meticulous work on his cabinets.

Visitors to the cabin report the continued presence of the old man, in a friendly, welcoming way. His spirit still lives there, greeting his guests.

Lynette tells the story of her own contacts with the cabin and its ghost.

"I was in there in 1977, and one of the guys that had a homestead out there on the Kanuti River was going out to work on a new addition," she said. "So a few of us gals who hung around the same group decided to go and help out. We would help chink logs, get the woodstove in, and set up a kitchen.

"That's when I first heard about Deadman's Camp.

"So one day I decided I was going to truck on over and just see what was over there. I got about fifteen or twenty feet from the place, and it was just like, warm. It was nice. Some places you walk up to and it's, 'Don't go in this building.' This said, 'Please come in.'

"I went in and nosed around inside and out. . . . It felt like somebody was there. I went over there about three or four times, and it was always like you expected somebody to walk in the door—the fellow that had the cabin, specifically—to show up, walk in the door, and put some tea on for you."

Adding to the strangeness of the region is an area that the Eskimos called Nuklani. It served as the dividing line between Inupiat Eskimos and Athabascan Indians: Eskimos were not permitted to go south of this point, and Indians could not go north of the line. Both Eskimos and Indians were killed in battles over this boundary. Nuklani is on one side of a ridge; on the other side, within the Indian territory, is Deadman's Camp.

## Tale End: Haunting the Bureaucracy

*The offices of the Alaska Department of Transportation in Anchorage are in a building that once served as a home for senior citizens. While employees carry out the work of the department, it seems that ghosts are busy trying to stake their own claim to the premises.*

*A few strange incidents have been reported from the rooms*

*and hallways of the government facility. There have been unexplained noises—tapping sounds, and footsteps when no one is present. Some people have reported the appearance of specters. Those who believe in such things speculate that the building's former residents are disgruntled over its transformation from senior citizens' home to bureaucratic headquarters.*

THE HOT SPRINGS LODGE SEEMS TO BE THE HOME OF PEOPLE LONG GONE WHO STILL CANNOT REST— GHOSTLY SPIRITS WHO SHOW UP AND WALK THE HALLS.

## An Air of Mystery

DRIVING INTO THE hamlet of Central in the Alaskan Interior, you might at first feel a sense of peace and tranquility. The Steese Highway winds for 125 miles east from Fairbanks into Central and the Circle Mining District, where gold was once king. It was near here in 1893 that gold was discovered by two prospectors named Pitka and Cherosky.

The old-timers have come and gone from that era, people like Jens Langlow, William Fee, Pie-faced Patsy, Three-fingered Bob, and Dutch Pete, all characters who carved out fame and fortune from the Alaskan wilderness.

All these men and women from Alaska's rich past have long since departed—or have they?

After you leave Central, a sign at Crabb's Corner will tell you that Circle Hot Springs is eight miles farther down the dusty gravel road. The road also heads to places like Deadwood, Harrison, and Ketchum, where miners still seek gold. Not much goes on here in the quiet mining district of today, but every once in a while someone will check in from the hills, and you could swear you were looking at a piece of the past.

Something strange is going on at Circle Hot Springs. It is apparently the home of people long gone who still cannot rest— ghostly spirits who show up and walk the halls of old buildings. They occupy the rooms where visitors lay their heads at night.

I was first exposed to the soothing waters of Circle Hot Springs in the late 1950s. As a small boy I spent part of each summer at my father's gold mining camp near Mastodon Creek in the Circle Mining District. My mother would haul me and my brothers and sisters to the hot springs for an occasional dip in the log-sided swimming pools. We spent many nights in one or another of the wooden cottages along the road, which looked a century old even back in the '50s.

I can attest to the creakiness and the air of mystery in these ancient abodes. But youngsters often see this sort of thing as fun— never realizing that someone might be watching. We never met a ghost, but as I learned later, not everyone can say that.

Circle Hot Springs was discovered in the fall of 1897 by George Growe while he was out hunting. Growe, a gold prospector, wounded a moose and trailed him for miles. The moose crossed a small stream, which Growe noticed was warm, and he traced the stream to its source at the hot springs.

The following April, Growe returned to the springs. While there, he found some wild plants that looked edible, so he cooked and ate them. The roots were poisonous. Growe became violently ill and later died.

The hot springs eventually became part of the 160-acre

homestead of Frank Leach, who had moved into the mining district in 1906, and his wife Emma. A nearby cemetery became the supposed final resting place for people who died in the area. No one knows exactly how many people were buried there; some headstones are missing. But the Leaches were put in the ground there, along with some of the gold miners from the old days on Portage Creek. The French Canadian fellow who pulled out his teeth and made a set of wooden ones is also buried there.

Susan Knapman, former operator of Circle Hot Springs, is a person who has heard many stories of the ghosts from the people who work there. She even has a few spooky experiences of her own to tell about.

"When my company took over the hot springs in 1991, they could hardly wait to tell me all the ghost stories," she said. "When I first got here, they were saying things like: 'Things would come flying off the shelf.'"

One of the workers caught a glimpse of a ghost and identified it as Emma Leach.

"We had a fur coat that hung in the basement," Susan said, "and one night our worker went down to get something and the fur coat reached out and touched her."

Susan said one of the cooks kept seeing a delicate, gossamer-like image, a kind of ghostly presence, though she couldn't make out any specific features.

Lingering footsteps have been often heard from certain rooms in which no one is staying.

One place a ghost likes to roam is the third-floor library. You'll find all sorts of books here, including mysteries and science fiction. It's a quaint library, with odd-shaped windows that let in light from the midnight sun.

"We had a big project to put some of the old books from one of the cabins in the library so they could be used," Susan said. "We had a person who worked as a teacher in the Fairbanks School District going through the books. She really worked hard at this. One day she got really frustrated. She was trying to eliminate or cull the books out and put them in a sack, only to find someone would move the sack.

"Finally, she could handle it no longer. She turned around to nothing and said, 'Mrs. Leach, I am not going to hurt the library, I just want to put it in shape!' After that she had no more problems."

At the hot springs, things go bump in the night. A rap at the door or a tap on the window have some patrons looking around, only to find no one there. Perhaps it was a visitation from Mrs. Leach.

Shortly after Susan Knapman first came to the hotel, she was in bed in her room on the first floor when she heard a knock on the door. She checked, and no one was there. The knocks continued. She finally decided she could do nothing about it, and if the knocker wanted something, it was welcome to come in. But nothing else happened, and she went back to sleep.

Winter at the hot springs can be dark, cold, and lonely. It takes a certain type of person to live this quiet life, and when things are quiet, much is noticed, especially the unusual occurrences. You tend to notice activity more when you think you're alone.

One night during a particularly cold winter, one of the workers looked outside and saw the ghostly image of a man playing a piano. It was 50 degrees below zero. Could it have been that nice little Irishman who worked there in the 1940s? He had a heart attack and fell over dead on the hood of his pickup truck in the parking lot. He was the bartender and dishwasher, and old-timers say he played the piano real well.

Susan's granddaughter lived with her at Circle Hot Springs from the time the girl was seven months old until she was two and a half. She had an imaginary friend that she talked to, a friend she called Ethel.

"How a child would pick up the name Ethel, I wouldn't know," Susan said. "But there was a lovely lady who was a desk clerk here for many years. She was an older lady and she really liked the hot springs.

She died a very violent death in her eighties in Seattle. Strangely enough, her name was Ethel."

One cold winter day, the daughter of one of the workers was playing cards in the main lobby with an old woman. The girl later told her father about the old lady, but it turned out that no such person was listed in the hotel register and there was no evidence that she even existed. Perhaps Ethel enjoyed cards.

Emma Leach breathed her last in room 312 at the hot springs lodge. According to many who stay in the room, strange things go on in the night. Doors become unexplainably locked or unlocked, or sometimes open by themselves.

People in cabin 10 at the hot springs also tell of unexplained incidents.

Maintenance man Mike Holland had his own ghostly encounter in 1995. It was nighttime, and Mike was down in the maintenance shop—the former shower room for the hot springs. It still reeks of sulfur from the hot springs, and many a bather once showered and passed through here.

Mike walked down a hallway to get an item he needed. At each side of the hallway was a small room.

"A person walked from my right to my left," Mike said. He thought it was a co-worker named Al, but unknown to him, Al had left work early that night.

"I nonchalantly talked with the person for a while, thinking it was Al, but I received no answer back.

"What I saw was not out of the corner of my eye or anything like that. I clearly saw this person walk across the hall from one room to the next. . . . The person didn't float, it walked."

Mike said the person was wearing pants, but he couldn't tell for sure whether it was a man or woman. He searched the rooms, expecting to find Al. There was no one. He realized he was the only living person in the place.

"There was no possible way anything or anyone could have gotten past me, because there was no way out of the rooms except past me," he said.

Then Mike remembered Al had told him that at times, he felt like he was being watched.

That wasn't the end of it for Mike Holland. He was picking out some rags from a box in the shop one day, then left for a few minutes. He returned to find someone going through the rag box. Mike asked what the man was doing. The man, holding rags in his hands, looked up at Mike, and suddenly vanished.

"It was like he dissolved into thin air," Mike said.

The stories go on and on, but they all seem to have happy endings. Susan says these are friendly ghosts: "We kind of think that someone is looking out for Circle Hot Springs, and if we're doing things right, they don't get upset."

People who stay at the hot springs have written notes to the ghost, but none have been answered, yet.

"In the bar, a bottle of beer will occasionally travel down the bar and slowly tip over," Susan said. "Everybody's eyes are wide open in disbelief. When it happens, they don't reach for it, they just watch it occur. There is no way, scientifically, we can explain that."

## Tale End: The Disappearing Woman

*In the late 1970s, a woman was killed in a car wreck that occurred near a gravel pit close to Trapper Creek, on the Parks Highway. Ever since then, witnesses say, a woman can occasionally be seen walking along the highway at this site. When she is approached, she disappears. Watch for her especially in the early morning hours.*

A CARETAKER WAS HIRED TO STAY AT THE CAMP

DURING THE INVESTIGATION, BUT HE LEFT IN FRIGHT.

HE HEARD TOO MANY NOISES AROUND THE CABIN

# Murder Most Foul

SOMETHING HORRIBLE took place in the Cache Creek Mining District in 1939. According to Dennis Garrett, who owns the mining claims where this incident took place, an eerie residue of this horror remains there yet today. The people whose lives were taken prematurely continue to have a stake in these claims.

The intriguing story unfolded in the fall of 1939. Concerns arose when F. W. Jenkins and his wife, Helen, failed to arrive back in Talkeetna as usual in the fall, after the mining season ended. Then came the headlines in the newspapers—about miners Dick Francis, Joy Brittell, and the Jenkins couple being brutally murdered on their Cache Creek claims.

At first the authorities thought Francis had killed everyone, then shot himself.

Miner Xan Clark of Talkeetna found the body of Francis after he passed by the Francis cabin and called out, but got no answer. Clark opened the door and found Francis on the floor, lying in a pool of blood. He had been shot in the head, and there was a revolver in his hand.

Francis had been in the region for more than thirty years. His cabin was about three miles from the nearest neighbor, and a pilot had dropped food supplies to him just a week earlier.

About a mile from the Francis cabin, on a trail leading to the residence of John Clark, the bodies of F. W. Jenkins and Joy Brittell were found. Brittell's foot protruded from beneath the grass and leaves that had been used to cover the bodies. The men had been beaten to death.

Dick Francis owned three dogs, and they were now pressed into service to haul the bodies five miles across the snow to the Jenkins cabin.

The body of Helen Jenkins was found about 150 feet from the Jenkins cabin on Ruby Gulch. Searchers found her body hidden in a growth of grass overhanging a gravel bank. It was determined she had been beaten to death. Pockets in her clothing were turned inside out, and this was taken as proof that robbery was a motive in the killings.

The investigation turned up five thousand dollars worth of gold dust hidden in the Jenkins cabin, perhaps the summer's diggings for the couple. Then an additional stash was found, valued at fifteen hundred dollars.

It was discovered that Dick Francis had two bullet holes in his head, eliminating the possibility of suicide.

Talkeetna residents said the Jenkins couple were very successful miners, and that they probably brought in far more than five thousand dollars worth of gold during a summer. They had been known to stash large amounts of gold around their cabin or nearby in the hills, until they could haul it out in the fall. Some gold was even found in a cabin they owned in Talkeetna.

Many people believe more gold still lies hidden in Ruby Gulch.

The murders are talked about yet today by local old-timers, and they remain one of Alaska's unsolved mysteries.

A caretaker was hired to stay at the Jenkins camp during the investigation, but he left in fright. He heard too many noises around the cabin—and he couldn't forget that a killer was still on the loose.

Dennis Garrett entered this one-time valley of death in 1985, to mine gold from the claims that he had secured. At the time he didn't know about the murders. But for some odd reason, he felt a strangeness upon entering the area, something he couldn't quite identify.

"There was something about the place," he told author Roberta Sheldon, who interviewed him for her book *The Mystery of the Cache Creek Murders.* "It caused a feeling I can't describe, like a wave or something that started in my feet and moved up. My hair prickled, and I thought, *Whoa—what's going on here.* I had a shotgun with me and brought it up because I felt threatened. I can still feel the hackles rising again just thinking about it."

## The Phantom Cat Train

THE CAT TRAIN has played a significant role in oil exploration in the frozen north. A cat train consists of a bulldozer pulling several trailers of supplies cross-country between camps, the trailers sitting on long iron sleds that glide over the tundra. Much of the cat train activity occurs in the darkest part of winter.

It was the winter of 1969 when oil-field worker Red Cooney was running a cat train from the North Slope to a remote exploration camp in eastern Alaska on the edge of the Brooks Range. With the northern lights dancing across the skies, Red enjoyed the peacefulness of being alone out on the isolated landscape. He'd occasionally stop his rig to watch the spectacular aurora displays.

Sometime during the night, Red saw the lights of another bulldozer bouncing up and down across the tundra. From experience he knew the look of a bulldozer as it makes its way over the darkened land. There weren't too many cat trains in those days, zigzagging across the North Slope, and Red knew that no other train was operating in that area.

Red could see the lights of the bulldozer for several hours—and although he kept moving, he could never put any distance between himself and the other machine. It was too risky to turn his engine off in order to listen for the sounds of the other rig, because his engine might not start again in the frozen night.

The distant bulldozer never got any closer. When Red arrived at the exploration camp, he told his story about the eerie sighting. The people in camp knew exactly what he was talking about: they had witnessed the same thing off and on over the years. Red was not the first—or the last—to witness the phantom cat train roaming the tundra.

## Tale End: The Model T

*Not far from Ketchikan in Southeast Alaska, Jay Scott was a passenger in a vehicle that was traveling up a narrow logging road late one evening when he saw headlights approaching. As they got nearer, the people in the vehicle saw that it was a Model T car, and it was careening right toward them.*

*The driver of Jay's vehicle tried to steer out of the way, but had no place to turn. They waited tensely for the collision. As they braced themselves, the old vehicle drove right on through them.*

*Jay said he felt a cold presence as the car passed through. He said he could clearly see expressions of terror on the faces of the occupants of the Model T.*

*It was a long, slow drive back to Ketchikan that night, with the group hardly believing what they had experienced.*

# The Hairy Man of Iliamna

FOR A GREAT many years, something has been roaming the hills, valleys, and villages of the Iliamna region of Southwestern Alaska.

Some say it's a ghost; other say it's Hairy Man.

Hairy Man is a Bigfoot-like creature that roams certain parts of Alaska. As in most places of the world, Alaska is home to creatures elusive to humans. Though no physical proof has been offered, eyewitness accounts tell of unusual events.

What Gus Jensen experienced one dark night at his cabin in the Iliamna region would make anyone's hair stand on end. Gus encountered something he'll never forget, and he still feels the pain of that frightful night.

Gus and his wife were sleeping in their bed that night when something came into the cabin and tried to drag him out. Gus Jensen had fought with many men, but this being was stronger than any man he had ever tangled with.

The creature began to drag him from the cabin, but Gus got wedged across the doorway. The thing started jerking on him, dislocating his shoulder and breaking bones. Gus's wife sprang to her husband's defense, shooting at the creature with a rifle. At that, the attacker let go and fled.

Gus Jensen's son Vern also had a run-in with Hairy Man, or something like it. He was trapping in the Pedro Bay area with Billy Vaudrin, and they were spending the nights at an abandoned cabin—despite warnings from villagers to steer clear. It was a bad place, the villagers said.

The four rooms in the rectangular cabin were laid out end to end. They picked out the best of the four rooms and made it into their temporary home, moving the stove into that room and fixing broken windows by using good windows from the rest of the cabin.

Vaudrin and Jensen were running the trapline by dog team. The men were at the cabin one night, sitting inside and mending dog harnesses. All of a sudden Vaudrin looked across the room to see that Jensen's eyes were wide with surprise as he stared at the window above Vaudrin's head.

Vaudrin leaned forward and looked back in time to see a hairy face and a hand disappear from the window. The men grabbed their guns and ran outside. But they found no tracks. Even more strange was the fact that the dogs were not disturbed.

Villagers had told Vaudrin and Jensen what to expect in this cabin. They would hear silverware rattling in the kitchen, the villagers said, and they would hear a thumping noise like someone hitting the base log of the cabin with the butt end of an ax.

Sure enough, every night they began to hear the rattling of

silverware and the thumping on the base log. The men would jump up to investigate, but they never found a thing. It got to the point where they no longer felt threatened by the mystery visitor.

One night turned out to be oddly different. Vaudrin got up with his flashlight and gun to check out the rattling and thumping. He and Jensen then heard a noise—like the sound of liquid spraying against a wooden wall. And then a stream of steaming liquid flowed into the room from beneath the door of the adjoining room.

The door had been nailed shut, so the men ran outside and around the cabin to get into the room. They discovered that on the inside door, about four feet up off the floor, was a wet spot—as if a man had stood there to urinate. There were no tracks, and the dogs again remained undisturbed.

Bob Attla, the brother of dog-mushing legend George Attla, once related a Hairy Man story told by his father about the Huslia area. Sometime in the 1920s, a woman from the village disappeared. She was never found. Several years later, some village men who were out hunting saw the missing woman out on the tundra. They called to her, and she took off running.

The men managed to catch the woman and speak with her. She told them she had been living with Hairy Man. She said that she liked him and wanted to continue living with him. She pleaded with the men to not shoot Hairy Man if they ever saw him. The men let the woman go, and over the next decade, she was seen again from time to time, but always at a distance.

Joe Chucwuk, who was from Aliknigik, north of Dillingham, also told a story he had heard from his father. Hairy Man lived north of the village. Periodically the villagers would take a young woman to that area and leave her there for Hairy Man. As long as they would do this, the story went, Hairy Man would not bother the village.

According to some old-timers, the village of Portlock was

abandoned because Hairy Man was killing off people there. It got so bad they had to move.

Alaska has had other sightings of Hairy Man, said to have taken place between Fairbanks and Nenana, just off the Parks Highway. Trappers and hunters have also reported Hairy Man up in the Knik Glacier area. All the stories are shrouded in mystery, and they continue to fascinate and intrigue generation after generation of Alaskans.

## The Sinrock Hills: Ghost Herder

THE INUPIAT ESKIMO known as Liolaes Charlie loved his work as a reindeer herder. He loved it so much that he couldn't bear to give it up when he died.

Alaska has a long history of reindeer herding, and the Seward Peninsula in Western Alaska was the grand herding grounds. Liolaes Charlie was from there—from the Sinrock Hills between Teller and Nome. It was the late 1800s, and Charlie felt a sense of pride and joy in a life of freedom, roaming as the reindeer did through the natural beauty of the area. It had been his life's ambition to tend the reindeer, and he became known for his love of life and of the herd he shepherded.

Then it was the year 1900, and an elderly Liolaes Charlie went to sleep one summer night, while the herd stood nearby in the thick moss of the Sinrock Hills off the Sinuk River. Liolaes Charlie passed away that night. He was buried according to the customs of the Eskimo people, but it wasn't long after his departure that strange things began to happen in the Sinrock Hills and to the herd of about four hundred reindeer.

Something kept scaring off the other herders, and the reindeer were left without a herdsman to watch over them. According to the herders, Charlie appeared to them night after night.

The herders were terrified. They said Charlie would appear and insist on sharing with them the vigils of the night. Even after death, he yearned to take on his herding responsibilities. These herders fled, and they couldn't be induced to return to the haunted herd.

They say that in the Sinrock Hills of the Seward Peninsula, the ghost of Liolaes Charlie still wanders in search of his reindeer herd.

## Tale End: The White House

*Yes, the White House is haunted, but not by Lincoln's ghost or by the ghosts of other presidents past. This White House is located in Skagway, Alaska, and is a bed and breakfast operated by John and Jan Tronrud.*

*This White House was built in 1902 by a saloon owner named R. L. Guthrie. It was a boarding house in the 1920s. During World War II, it was used as an officers' headquarters and hospital. It's now an immaculate structure that John Tronrud remodeled and restored after a fire in 1977.*

*"It has a lot of history," he said. "There's a possibility that someone died in the house and things started happening."*

*At the White House, things can go bump in the night. A worker there got glimpses of specters and experienced unexplained opening of doors. Every once in a while, someone will see a ghostly, fuzzy, white shape materialize briefly.*

*Once late at night, John Tronrud heard the front door open and someone walked upstairs. "I got out of bed and there was nobody around," he said.*

WHO HAUNTS THE RED ONION? SOME SAY IT'S THE ORIGINAL MADAM. OTHERS BELIEVE IT IS THE GHOST OF DELILAH, ONE OF THE LADIES OF THE NIGHT.

# The Spirited Brothel

THERE WAS A TIME when the Red Onion was known as the House of Negotiable Affection. Many a lonely man sought female companionship there during the days when the Southeast Alaska town of Skagway was the gateway to the Klondike goldfields.

The notorious Soapy Smith had his hand in the business. He made sure he and his gang had a piece of the action with the upstairs bordello. The Red Onion was also known for its nineteen-foot mahogany bar.

Move forward about eight decades, to 1978. The Red Onion was now a gift shop owned by Jan Wrentmore, and Lauri Rapuzzi worked in the shop. Wrentmore had just bought the property and had moved there from Juneau.

The building was a wooden structure in red and white, with double doors in front that opened out onto the sidewalk. Upstairs, Lauri recalls, "there were little rooms called cribs along both sides of the hallway, once used by the prostitutes. The cribs were just big enough for a twin bed, and hooks on the walls to hang garments."

In its heyday, the Red Onion displayed a row of dolls behind the bar. Each doll had the name of one of the working girls on it. When she was busy, the doll was put on its back. If she was available, the doll was set upright.

Lauri said that when she came to work at the gift shop, "there were certain rooms that we couldn't go into because the floorboards were so rotten that you'd fall through."

"We used to go upstairs occasionally in certain rooms to get different things," she said. "It was one of those things where you felt kind of creepy when you were upstairs. I was never really scared out of my wits, but we knew there was something living up there."

Lauri said that she her co-workers often would be downstairs working when they would hear someone walking around above them. And of course there would be no one there. Occasionally it sounded like the person, or thing, was dancing. A woman's laughter could be heard on occasion.

"There would be two or three other people working as salespeople with me and we'd be standing there and you could hear the footsteps walking around upstairs. I remember a couple of times when Mary or Velma would say, 'Is Jan upstairs?'

"Jan would have gone down for a bowl of soup or be gone to the post office. At least twice I had to go to the top of the stairs just to double-check and have a listen, and to make sure that somebody hadn't come in the back door."

"There was music once in a while," Lauri said, "like that tinny piano sound, the plinking of the keys, that old-time piano sound. . . . I never felt threatened, but I always felt like I wasn't completely alone in there."

The shop was designed to retain the aura of a gold-rush bordello, even to having mannequins in a couple of the cribs, dressed in period attire and illuminated by red lights. Windows in the cribs allowed a view from below in the street.

"If we wanted to we could dress up in old-time gold-rush garb," Lauri said. "I'd dress up once in a while, standing behind the counter looking like a tart. The ghost upstairs added to the fun of the job."

Who is it that haunts the Red Onion? Some say it's the original brothel madam. Others believe it is the ghost of Delilah, one of the ladies of the night who once worked there.

"I felt like it was a female presence," Lauri Rapuzzi said. "It was kind of creepy but I never felt threatened. I almost felt like there was a reverence. If these spirits had hung around that long for whatever reason, who am I to question? There's a sense of a little sadness perhaps. I'm sure these women led terrible, hard lives."

Whoever or whatever lives upstairs at the Red Onion apparently doesn't much care for men.

"We had one young man that worked with us," Lauri said. "He went up there a couple of times and said he didn't want to ever go up there again. He just felt overwhelmed by something that made him feel not welcome.

"One man was nearly shoved down the stairs. It was just because he wasn't supposed to be up there. As a rule, no men ventured upstairs."

## Baranof Castle: A Tragic Love Affair

THE TOWN OF SITKA is picturesque from every point of view, with its foreground of green islands and still waters and its backdrop of snowcapped mountains. The town's traditions and history invest it with much charm. The sad story of Princess Olga of Baranof Castle is an intriguing and mystifying piece of Sitka history.

The town site was established as a Russian outpost in 1799. This first Russian settlement was attacked by Natives and practically wiped out, but the second colony was more successful. In 1804, the Russians defeated the Natives in battle. The outpost was named Novo Arkhangelsk, for the archangel Michael, in hopes that the residents would receive his protection. (The town was later named Sitka, a Tlingit word meaning "by the sea.")

The Russians developed a busy outpost, with a flour mill, barracks, a fort, sawmill, tannery, a foundry, a shipbuilding plant, and a residence for Alexander Baranof, manager of the Russian-American Company and the first governor of Russian Alaska. Construction of Baranof Castle during the 1820s ushered in an era of great activity, with establishment of Lady Etolin's School, military and civilian installations, the Kirenski River Dam, and the Cathedral of St. Michael.

The officials of the colony lived a gay life at times, with great entertainment at the castle from about 1826 until 1833, when the deteriorating structure was torn down. A second castle was built in 1837 and was the site of much activity until the purchase of Alaska by the United States in 1867. A succession of charming ladies was brought to the castle to join in the lifestyle of the town's nineteenth-century upper class.

The Russian-American Company had its headquarters in the town, and in 1840 Colonel Eeolian was named the new chief manager and governor. He brought his Finnish bride with him. He was also serving as the sponsor of his niece, Princess Olga Feodorovna, after her parents died, and she too came to the colony. She was a young woman of some beauty, with large, dark eyes, and hair that was so black it seemed almost blue.

After a large Russian naval ship arrived at the outpost, many of the sailors became attracted to the princess. But only one caught her eye.

At the same time, a friend of the governor's arrived in town. He too fell under Olga's spell, and he told the governor—her uncle—that he wished to marry her. When the governor brought the man's case to Olga, she rejected it outright—because she had fallen in love with a lieutenant on the Russian ship.

The young couple began meeting at night along the Indian River. On a walk one evening, the governor spotted the couple. He left in haste and ordered the ship's captain to leave on a long voyage. And thus the lover was removed from the scene.

After that, Olga and her confidant, a nurse, went up to the cupola of the town's lighthouse every night, watching for the return of the ship.

The governor forced the marriage of his orphaned niece to his friend. Submissive and quiet, Princess Olga acquiesced in the wedding, which took place on March 18, 1844.

An enormous banquet was given after the wedding. As the bride sat, very solemn, a ship's horn was heard. The nurse ran in and whispered in Olga's ear that her lover's ship had returned. He was waiting outside her bedchamber.

She excused herself and left the banquet. At her bedchamber, the lovers embraced. Olga knew the situation was hopeless. In desperation, she pulled out the lieutenant's saber and plunged it into his heart, killing him, and then stabbed herself to death with it.

In the decades that followed, a succession of governors and their households occupied the castle. And with them came the stories told by people who stayed in the bedroom once used by Princess Olga: stories of seeing the Lady in Blue, the princess in her blue wedding gown and her silver crown. Some guests even said they talked with the princess.

Exactly fifty years after her death—on March 18, 1894—the

castle burned down, never again to be rebuilt. Some people think that hot tar being used in renovation of the castle caused the blaze. Others are convinced that the princess had returned to destroy the building that was the scene for her of so much grief.

## Tale End: The Ship That Vanished

*In 1973, three crewmen on the state ferry* Malaspina *observed a mysterious vessel, in an incident resembling accounts of the legendary* Flying Dutchman *ghost ship.*

*Early on a clear Sunday morning, the chief mate, along with two sailors, one at the lookout and one at the helm, were standing watch on the bridge. As the ferry moved toward Ketchikan, near Twin Island and Revillagigedo Channel, the men suddenly saw a huge, gray vessel about eight miles ahead, broadside and dead in the water.*

*For about ten minutes the men watched the ship and observed it as being exact, natural, and real. With binoculars they viewed sailors moving about on board. Suddenly the ship disappeared.*

THE GHOST WOKE JOHN STRANG ONE NIGHT
TO WARN HIM OF TROUBLE. THE GHOST TOLD HIM:
'JOHNNY, JOHNNY, WAKE UP!' NO ONE BUT HIS
MOM HAD EVER CALLED HIM JOHNNY.

# The Ghost Smoked a Pipe

NESTLED ALONG THE Copper River near the mouth of the Gakona
River, five miles east of Gulkana, is a beautiful log roadhouse. The
traveler who stops in for a meal and a tank of gas or to take a room for
the night admires the quaint old wagons, antiques, and other relics of
a bygone era. Like most roadhouses, now becoming extinct across
Alaska, the Gakona Roadhouse has a colorful history, with roots going
back to gold-rush days.

Most visitors have no idea that strange and unexplained events
occur amid the pleasant atmosphere of the roadhouse.

First, let's set the scene for the unfolding story of this haunted house.

In 1902, Felix Pedro discovered gold near Fairbanks. The find proved to be the richest in the Far North—richer than the Klondike, richer than Nome. In that same year, a man named Jim Doyle filed for a homestead at the present site of the Gakona Roadhouse. He built a single-story house to serve as a roadhouse. The Valdez Transportation Company acquired the property in 1905 and built a two-story log roadhouse.

Gakona was located in a strategic spot near the junction of the trails from Valdez to Eagle and from Valdez to Fairbanks. Valdez Transportation was already hauling large amounts of gold from Fairbanks. The company also had mail contracts for the routes between Valdez and Fairbanks and between Valdez and Eagle. The roadhouse was the scene of brisk business until around 1912, when the trail junction was moved. Manager George Rorer then turned the operation into more of a trading post than a roadhouse.

The business was later sold to Mike Johnson, who operated it until 1919 when it was taken over by J.M. Elmer, owner of the Slate Creek Mining Company. After 1926, the operation was leased to Arne Sundt, who later bought it and built a new lodge. He added to the new lodge as the demand for services grew, helped by the Nabesna Mine and eventually by construction of the Alcan Highway.

Sundt died suddenly in 1946. His wife Henra took over the roadhouse and continued to operate it until 1975, when she sold it to brothers John and Jerry Strang—who then learned they had purchased a roadhouse with an unexpected tenant.

As soon as the Strang families arrived, the action began. They were all sitting in the living room one winter evening, after a day of heavy snowfall. They were playing Monopoly when they heard the front door open and close. Heavy footsteps went across the lobby and stopped at the entry to the living room. The Strangs looked toward the entry, expecting to see someone. No one was there. The family dog went crazy, barking and running.

Jerry Strang's wife, Barbara, said the dog "ran up the stairs, and ran back and forth down the hall. . . . My husband went upstairs and looked everywhere and followed the dog. He looked everywhere and never found anybody."

She said that despite the fresh snow outside, "there were no tracks."

Curious things continued to happen. Doors would be locked from the inside, but there would be no one in the room. One room had a hook-and-eye fastener on the inside of the door, and somehow the hook dropped into the eye and secured the door shut. This occurred several times—and it doesn't happen by itself.

One day Barbara Strang was cleaning a bathroom across the hall from room 5. She heard a thumping and creaking of bedsprings from that room, like someone jumping up and down on the bed. But the room had not been rented.

Slowly she walked over to the door of room 5 and knocked. No one answered. She then went inside. No one was there. She decided to go back to cleaning the bathroom—but first she dashed down to the dining room and got one of the workers to help out and keep her company. The two went upstairs to finish the cleaning—but soon the sound of thumping and creaking bedsprings was heard again.

"It made my hair stand on end," Barbara said. But still no one could be found.

Barbara says they don't know for sure whose spirit inhabits the roadhouse. "We asked Henra Sundt about the ghost, and she said she didn't know about a ghost. She never had any unusual experiences."

One clue is that this ghost apparently smokes a pipe. The Strangs, non-pipe smokers all, experienced the unexplained aroma of pipe tobacco a number of times. While they were all seated at dinner one evening, the smell mysteriously wafted through the air.

A possible candidate as the Gakona ghost is a man who helped

Arne Sundt build the roadhouse. A photo shows a rather tall, large man with a tobacco pipe in one hand.

Barbara also said the ghost may have been a big person, because its footsteps are so heavy.

The year the Strangs restored the carriage house, which is now the restaurant, they spent a couple of months cleaning out the building. That winter, much ghostly activity took place. When things are moved, Barbara said, when changes are made, the ghosts appear. It's as if they don't like change.

"My brother-in-law John was living in the lodge at the time the restoration was taking place, and the carpenter that was helping in the building was staying upstairs. One morning they both got up, and John said to the carpenter: 'Who were you talking to downstairs?'

"'Well, I thought *you* were downstairs talking,' the carpenter said."

They both had heard voices, but no one else was around.

The ghost even woke John Strang one night to warn him of possible trouble. The ghost told him: "Johnny, Johnny, wake up!" No one but his mom had ever called him Johnny. As he awoke, he could see a stranger out in the lobby, standing there menacingly. The man had come through the back door in the middle of the night as everyone slept. John managed to chase him out of the building.

"It kind of seemed like the ghost was helping out," he said.

After that incident the Strangs believed the ghost might be a friend and a guardian.

"After all these years, I'm not so afraid of it," Barbara said. "Nothing that has happened here was bad or scary. One thing that's real hard about these old buildings and all the old places around here is they make so much noise anyway. A lot of things creak and sound like it could be a ghost."

One night as she was going to sleep, the bedroom door opened and she heard footsteps around the bed. In the morning she asked her husband if he had gotten out of bed in the night and walked around. He hadn't. He had been sound asleep because of the medicine he took for a bad cold. They chalked it up to another ghostly visitation.

Barbara was alone in the kitchen one day, working as she listened to music on the old eight-track stereo system. She walked to the bar to get some ice, but when she returned, she heard only silence. All the function knobs on the stereo had been turned down, including the volume. Who did it? Apparently nothing human.

A woman and her son were once staying upstairs when they ran down to report that the lodge was on fire. They had seen smoke billowing from the walls and the floor. But it didn't have any odor. The Strangs checked upstairs and found nothing.

Then there was the young woman who was afraid of the dark.

"One time my niece was here," Barbara related. "She was about twenty-one and grew up being afraid of the dark.

"When she first got here, she was supposed to sleep up in the attic. One night she was going to bed, and she kept the curtains open when she slept. She turned off a ceiling light next to the door and turned on a lamp next to the bed, getting ready to read a magazine. Suddenly the light went out and the curtain closed!

"She slept down with our eight-year-old daughter that night."

All the hauntings at the Gakona Roadhouse have occurred in the current restaurant or lodge. The Strangs haven't spent a lot of time in the old, original roadhouse, which still stands, deserted and forlorn looking. They don't know if it's haunted too, and they're not all that anxious to find out.

"It's spooky just going over to the old roadhouse and looking at it," Barbara said. "Last time we were over there we found old letters and other stuff, including a piece of furniture from the old post office. The building was making noises and creaks and groans and was not comfortable."

She summed up life with their resident phantom: "We're just kind of used to the ghost and it's a good ghost, and we want to keep it that way."

## Tale End: The Crying of Children

*Many people feel uncomfortable on the fourth floor of the Mount Edgecombe Hospital in Sitka. It has a reputation for being haunted. Over the years, workers have heard bumping sounds, seen flickering lights, and heard footsteps—with no obvious explanation of what caused them.*

*The hospital is a former public-health sanitarium, and the dying were cared for on the fourth floor. Among the patients were children dying of tuberculosis, once a dread disease. Some people believe these children can still be heard crying.*

'WHO ARE YOU?' ELIN ASKED. THERE WAS NO REPLY.

IN AN INSTANT, THE FIGURE TOOK OFF DOWN

THE HALL, ROTATING AS IT WENT, THEN VANISHED.

# Apparitions of the Air

IF YOU'RE EVER in Anchorage visiting the Alaska Aviation Heritage Museum, you might see more than historical displays. Some say the museum can take on a life of its own, with strange occurrences that might send chills up your spine. And I don't mean the kind of chills you get from the wind of a propeller.

The museum reflects the history of aviation in Alaska, and this history means much more than just airplanes. Each aircraft on display there had its occupants, the people who once flew them—people like famed bush pilot Ben Eielson.

Museum worker Ingrid Pedersen, one of Alaska's past great

women pilots, has had unusual experiences there that she won't soon forget. On a dark November afternoon, Ingrid was alone in the museum, preparing to leave for the day, when she heard firm, heavy footsteps coming up the hallway. She figured it was a worker from the nearby hangar.

The footsteps stopped right behind a corner of the doorway to the room she was in.

"Come right in," Ingrid said.

There was no answer.

She walked a few steps to the doorway and peered down the hall. There was no one there. She sat down—and once more heard the footsteps. Grabbing a stapler as a makeshift weapon, she quietly walked to the door and waited. The steps came closer and closer, then stopped right outside the door, just out of view.

She worked up enough nerve to step outside of the room. Again, no one was in the hall. Now she was uneasy, with nervous thoughts racing through her mind. Perhaps it was an intruder.

Then she remembered the words of museum director Ted Spencer, when she first came to work at the museum.

"There are ghosts here," Spencer had said. "I think it might be Ben Eielson walking around once in a while."

She heard the steps once more, starting outside the area that displays aviation history from World War II and the Aleutian Islands. Then she heard someone, or something, moving through a gate that separates the museum offices from the public area.

Ingrid quickly ran out the door. This time she didn't dare look down the hall. She made it down the stairs, out the main door, and safely into her car. Looking up at the office windows from her car, she half-expected to see something staring back at her.

Suddenly Ingrid felt foolish, almost embarrassed. Maybe she was imagining all this.

A bright sun was shining the next day as she returned to work.

Inside, the museum was in semi-darkness, with only the soft lights of the exhibits. Ingrid stopped to talk with Laurie Woodard, manager of the museum's gift shop. She decided to tell Laurie what had happened the day before.

As Ingrid was relating her experience, a tall, dark, slim shape dashed from the main exhibit and ran across the hallway into the theater.

"What was that?" Ingrid asked. "I saw a dark figure running across the hall."

"I know," Laurie said. "I've seen it too. But even worse, I hear steps upstairs when I know very well that no one except me is at the museum."

Ingrid Pedersen's daughter-in-law, Elin, had her own strange encounter at the museum. Elin Pedersen comes from an island on the Norwegian coast, where legend says there are gnomes and trolls hiding in cellars and mountain caves. Elin was leaving a rest room at the museum when she was confronted with a gray, indistinct figure, about four feet tall. This apparition, wearing what appeared to be a top hat, looked up at her with an expression of worry on its face.

"Who are you?" Elin asked as she stepped backward. There was no reply. In an instant, the figure took off down the hall, rotating as it went, then vanished.

Elin also reported hearing footsteps upstairs after closing time, and the sound of someone jumping onto the floor from some height.

Sylvia Kavinsky, a summer museum assistant, also heard footsteps while she was alone at the museum and all the doors were locked. Sylvia was working at the copy machine when she heard the footsteps approaching.

"I don't want to see you!" she shouted. The steps stopped. She ran in terror from the museum and found her boyfriend, who was working at the nearby airport. The pair returned to the museum, but nothing was amiss, and they closed up for the night.

Sylvia also tells about a young traveler from Arizona who had permission to spend the night on the gift shop floor. He couldn't get to sleep. He was kept awake by the sound of footsteps and other noises around the museum. Finally he made sure the entry to the gift shop was locked, and he waited for the dawn, greatly relieved when daylight finally arrived.

Ted Spencer says he has heard objects being moved around in certain rooms of the museum—and then has found nothing disturbed when he went to investigate.

"It's no fun at all to unlock a room, where you hear lots of noise, and find everything in order, no one there," he said. "And every time, I feel I am being watched, something is quietly watching."

The exhibit on World War II includes many photos of Japanese and American military personnel. In one especially haunting photo, a Japanese soldier looks straight at the viewer. Ingrid Pedersen tells of a woman who was at the museum to look into the stories of the ghost. She knew the stories and had been researching them. She took one look at the photo of the Japanese aviator and cried out, "It's him, it's him!"

## Tale End: The Restless Miner

*Many old-timers have come and gone along the streams and in the hills of the Fortymile region of eastern Alaska, people like Buckskin Miller, Sam Patch, and George Matlock. But it seems that some of those who passed on aren't quite ready to leave just yet.*

*Along Steel Creek, a tributary of the Fortymile River, a mining camp dating back to the 1890s can still be seen. In the heyday of the Fortymile mining district, miners took out thousands of ounces of gold from area claims. On Jack Wade Creek, miners turned up nuggets as large as fifty-four ounces.*

*The mining camp of Steel Creek, about forty miles south
of Eagle, had a post office, general store, and roadhouse. It also
boasted a U.S. marshal and ferry service. Through the years, an
old cabin at one mining claim has been the scene of numerous
unsettling events experienced by prospectors, hikers, and adventurers.*

*A couple once decided to spend the winter in the cabin. They
cut their stay short after they heard someone walking outside,
crunching across the crisp frozen landscape, even though no one
could be seen.*

*In other incidents, someone would walk from the woods,
come up to the doorstep, and stop at the front door. Of course no
one would be there. One time, footprints were found that led out
through the woods, but they quickly ended in nothing. On other
occasions, someone could be heard walking at night through the
trees and around the cabin. No ghost has ever materialized;
people only hear sounds or see footprints.*

*Perhaps one of these prospectors of the past still longs to mine
the gold-rich gravels of the rivers and streams of the Fortymile.*

I GOT INTO BED THAT FIRST NIGHT,

BUT I WOKE UP AT MIDNIGHT, SCREAMING.

IT WAS THE SAME DREAM, EXACTLY!

# Nightmare of the Past

ABOUT FIFTEEN HUNDRED miles out on Alaska's Aleutian Island chain, the village of Atka sits between Korovin and Nazan Bay, in the shadow of the Korovin Volcano. Residents are mostly Aleut natives. Aleuts have lived here for centuries, living off the rich sea life in nearby bays and along the rocky coast. It was in this isolated, historic village that I experienced my own personal nightmarish encounter with the unknown.

Atka has a long and difficult history. It was once known for the artistic baskets and grass mats woven by the Native women. The men of Atka were good hunters, and the plentiful sea otters were their favorite prey.

Then the Russians arrived. The Russians nearly exterminated the sea otters in their quest for fur, and they forced the Aleuts into subservience, submitting them to rape and murder. Perhaps the terror of those years still lives on at Atka.

In 1972, Alaska journalist Lael Morgan went to Atka on a Rockefeller Foundation grant to document the transition of Alaska Natives from a subsistence to a money economy. The following is the remarkable story of her experiences there, told in her voice:

When I visited Atka, the only way there was by a Coast Guard ship, which pulled in once each month. On my visit, the ship missed its return trip—so I stayed for two months. About ninety people were living in the village at the time.

I stayed in the residence of the priest, who came to the village for only one month each year. Otherwise the building next to the Russian Orthodox church stood empty. I was thrilled. The residence was painted in pretty pastels. It was a beautiful house with lots of rooms.

This lovely place seemed to be just what I needed. I was in a bad emotional state after breaking up with my fiancé. I was also a bit afraid of being in Atka, a place I had been warned about. I was told (incorrectly) that I might be in danger from drunken residents.

I don't dream often, but on my first night in Atka, I had a dream. Or perhaps I should say a nightmare. I dream in color, and I dreamed of a primitive battle scene. I didn't notice any particular race of people or any special kind of clothing or uniform. But there was a hell of a battle going on, and I was right in the middle of it. Arms and legs were flying everywhere, and blood was all over the place.

That dream repeated itself every night. I started asking people if something horribly violent had happened near Atka—something that might somehow have prompted my dream. They said no. But Atka is an ancient place, and the Aleuts were often at war with one another.

Wherever you have a long-inhabited site in the Aleutians, it's likely that somebody fought over it.

At the end of the second week, in the middle of the night, I got up and grabbed my bedding and moved to a couch in the living room. And I never had the dream again. Instead, I began to experience a bit of unexplained magic. I would make up the couch neatly each morning and push it out of the way into a corner. But when I returned later in the day, the couch would be in the middle of the room. The next morning I would again push it into the corner, but when I returned, it would have taken its same little walk. This is earthquake country, and I wondered if tiny quakes were causing the couch to move. But no one I talked with had any similar experiences.

I returned the following year, on assignment to do a story on the village for *National Geographic* magazine. By then I had patched up my differences with my fiancé, and life was great. I stayed again at the priest's residence.

I got into bed that first night, but I woke up at midnight, screaming. It was the same dream, exactly! Again I took to my sleeping couch, and the dream never returned.

About two years later I was talking with a businessman I know—a scientific, no-nonsense guy. I had told him about my stays in the priest's residence—about my recurring dream and about the walking couch. He told me that he also had stayed in the priest's residence during a visit to Atka.

"Did you hear what happened to me?" he asked.

I was startled to hear his story. He and two other people were staying at the house, and they were using a gas heater to warm the place while they slept. The man woke to discover that carbon monoxide was escaping from the heater, and that the other two people were unconscious. He crawled to the door and opened it, then returned to save the two people.

"Now do you believe me when I say that place is haunted?"
I asked him.

"No," he replied.

"Would you go back?" I asked.

His reply was emphatic. "I'll never go back in that place again!"

## Wickersham House: The Judge Loved Bacon

JAMES WICKERSHAM wore many hats in his illustrious career
during Alaska's maturing as a U.S. territory. He was a judge, lawyer,
delegate to Congress, explorer, and author. As a judge, Wickersham
was responsible for the 300,000-square-mile Third Judicial District.
In 1903 he led the first attempt to climb Mount McKinley. He
even continued to make his presence known after his death.

Evangeline Atwood, in her book *Frontier Politics*, said of
Wickersham:

> "No other man has made as deep and varied imprints
> on Alaska's heritage, whether it be in politics, government,
> commerce, literature, history or philosophy."

Wickersham bought a house in Juneau in 1928 and lived there
with his wife, Grace, until he died in 1939. Wickersham had a book
collection with thousands of volumes, which he displayed on rows
of shelves in the house. The building later became the property of
Ruth Allman, step-niece of Wickersham. She sold it in 1974 to
Robert Geirsdorf, who sold it ten years later to the State of Alaska.
The house was then made into apartments.

One of Wickersham's favorite meals when he lived in this house
consisted of bacon and eggs. In the years since the judge's death,
occupants of the house or visitors have smelled bacon cooking,

the aroma floating through the rooms of the old place. They have searched in vain for the source of the smell.

Wickersham himself has been observed in brief encounters.

Grace Wickersham lived for many years after her husband's death, and it was said that the judge was waiting all that time for her to join him. After she passed away, the ghostly activity slowed down, and visitations were not as frequent. The presence of perfume wafting through the air has been on the list of unusual occurrences at the house.

Musician Pat Wendt once visited the house on a Sunday afternoon, and he was treated to stories about the ghost of Wickersham—and to a personal encounter with the unexplainable.

"We were sitting around the table in a parlor area and there were a few musicians and we were having a jam session," Pat said. "Between songs we started talking about the ghosts of Wickersham house. Of course they told me about how he hung around as long as she was alive. It was reported several times he was seen in various spots through the house or in his study upstairs. One would see a profile and one more look and he'd be gone.

"We played another song and we were just chatting, and the smell of bacon cooking wafted through the air."

Pat and the others began searching for the source of the odor, but to no avail.

"Everyone could smell it," Pat said. "We walked around the house, looked outside, everywhere we could look. Every nook and cranny we looked and could not find any cooking bacon.

"It was a distinct odor of bacon, very very strong. We were all going *ooooh*. It definitely validated the ghost stories they were telling."

Some witnesses have seen old Wickersham himself sitting at his desk, staring out the window over Juneau. Occasionally footsteps are heard upstairs, undoubtedly the restless judge pacing the floor and contemplating how well his bacon is cooked.

## Tale End: No Place to Spend a Night

*The old four-story Tonsina Roadhouse looms up off the Richardson Highway, near the Tonsina River. Its windows are dark, and the place has been closed for quite some time. It's not a cheery sight.*

*A few brave souls have gotten permission to spend the night in the old place, but some have reported they could sleep only fitfully. Passersby swear they have seen a strange-looking figure standing at a window and peering out.*

*The Mangy Moose Saloon near the roadhouse is another site of unsettling events. The original owner, Bill Ogden, committed suicide many years ago. Since then, the image of Ogden, wearing a brim hat, has been seen in the mirror of the bar. And some folks claim they've seen him walking through the barroom.*

THE BROTHERS MAY HAVE DISCOVERED
A RICH LODE BEFORE THEY DIED. IN THE
SEARCH FOR THIS MISSING BONANZA, MORE THAN
TWO DOZEN MEN HAVE LOST THEIR LIVES.

# Headless Valley

WELCOME TO HEADLESS VALLEY—a place named for the two unfortunate miners who were found beheaded in this deep, foreboding river valley in Canada's Northwest Territories.

For nearly a century, this valley has been said to be haunted. The strangest of events have occurred here. Many people have ventured into the valley, never to return. Some of the disappearances could be explained; others couldn't.

Since 1906, when the McLeod brothers' skeletal remains were

found tied to trees, their heads missing, prospectors have been going into this Nahanni River valley in search of gold. It is believed that the brothers discovered a rich lode before they died. In this search, more than two dozen men have lost their lives.

The Nahanni is a wild river, with such a powerful current that most travelers portage around the many rapids. Virginia Falls on the Nahanni River, at 317 feet high, is one of the world's great waterfalls. The Nahanni is beautiful but deadly.

Those who survive a journey into the valley in search of gold talk about the strange effect the valley can have on the mind. Some who have been there speak of magnificence and majesty. Others simply call it Witch Country, or Deadmen Valley, or Headless Valley.

The valley is at the southern end of the Mackenzie Mountains, about two hundred miles north of Fort Nelson; access is by plane, or by boat up the Liard River. Like a beast lying in wait, the Headless Valley welcomes its prey. There are stories of a group of prospectors from Europe vanishing in the early 1960s; of a body found washed ashore below the great falls. Camps have been found with remnants of human bones, and mining equipment scattered around. It's as if someone wants the valley to himself.

Some of the deaths were investigated. In certain cases, scurvy was to blame for prospectors' deaths. Starvation and drowning were other causes of death. But murder has also played a defining role in Headless Valley.

Eno and Willie McLeod first set out prospecting in 1904. They came up through British Columbia and parts of Southeast Alaska, arriving in the Nahanni River country. They ended up on the upper Flat River, where they found Dogrib Indians in possession of coarse gold nuggets, some as large as a quarter-ounce in size.

The McLeods made camp next to a stream they named Gold Creek. The Indians apparently had already removed the best of the gold, leaving little for the brothers. From the creek, the two men extracted only ten ounces of gold, which they kept in a moosehide bag.

The brothers decided to head for Fort Liard, which would mean a long run down the Flat and Nahanni Rivers and then an eighty-mile trip up the Liard River. They built a crude wooden boat for running the rivers, but the boat swamped in Flat River Canyon. They lost everything except the bag of gold.

They returned to Gold Creek, where they panned briefly for more gold. They had better luck with their second attempt to travel down the rivers. This time they made a rope from strips of moosehide, to use in lowering the boat down the worst places in the river. They finally made it through the canyon and down to the Liard River, then upstream to Fort Liard.

The following year, the brothers set out again in search of gold, traveling to the place along the Nahanni River that later became known as Headless Valley. It was now 1905, and the McLeods' camp was located among spruce trees on the banks of the Nahanni.

A notation written by one of the brothers was later discovered, and it said: "We have found a fine prospect."

A few trappers and hunters in the area said that before the brothers were killed, they saw a third man with the McLeods. This third man was later seen selling gold at several trading posts. He showed up at Telegraph Creek in British Columbia, and was eventually traced by the Mounted Police to Vancouver. It was estimated that he was carrying about eight thousand dollars in gold nuggets. He was never apprehended.

It was 1906 before the McLeod brothers were found, headless, tied to trees. They were found by their brother Charlie, who buried the men and placed a cross to mark their graves. Their murders have never been solved.

In the late 1920s, the McLeod story took a strange twist. Several men in the area were found murdered, and a couple more disappeared. Suspicions were directed at Albert Johnson, a loner who lived in a crude log cabin and who was among the many who had been searching for the lost McLeod gold mine.

Johnson was wanted for stealing from traplines, and he shot a Mountie who tried to confront him at his cabin. Johnson was finally cornered up on the Eagle River in northern Yukon Territory on the border of the Northwest Territories, where he died in a shootout with Canadian authorities. In his possession were gold teeth that had extracted from the mouths of prospectors who had been found dead in Headless Valley.

A large portion of the Nahanni River, including Headless Valley, is now part of Canada's Nahanni National Park. And the lost McLeod gold mine is still lost.

## The Mendeltna Lodge: Bonnie the Friendly Ghost

THE MENDELTNA LODGE, along the Glenn Highway at Milepost 153, has a lot to offer visitors. The clear, cold Mendeltna River flows nearby, with grayling and salmon that attract visitors for fishing during the summer. You'll find the usual amenities at the lodge: comfortable rooms in an old log building, several cabins, a barroom with a stone fireplace, plus a big campground.

There are also a couple of attractions that are not so usual, such as the lodge's Drunken Forest Museum, a collection of peculiar trees. But the most intriguing feature of all is the resident known as Bonnie. Bonnie the ghost.

Cindy Lockert has worked at the lodge for more than a decade, and she has seen a lot of activity from Bonnie the ghost.

"There was one day where . . . all of a sudden my cook comes running out to the big dining room. I had heard our dishwasher start up and I knew that Steve never did start the dishwasher. . . . I told him it was Bonnie, our ghost."

"It wasn't long after that, another neighbor came in and he was sitting at a table here in the kitchen, just reading a newspaper, and all of a sudden our washing machine fired up in the back room. We knew that Carol Adkins, the owner of the lodge, wasn't up yet." It was Bonnie, hard at work again.

"Bonnie's a friendly ghost, but she just does things in a mischievous way," Cindy said. Like the time Bonnie apparently decided to make two pots of coffee, at the same time. So she just dumped extra water into the coffeemaker.

"I came back from the big dining room, and nobody else had poured in another pot of water, and there was coffee running out our back door."

Bonnie also likes to slam doors. The doors at the lodge are heavy, and when they slam shut, you know it. "You'll be here and it's nice and quiet, and you'll hear the doors open and slam," Cindy said. "We're used to it. It doesn't scare us."

Adkins named the ghost, but no one really knows who she might have been. "Carol Adkins says the ghost likes her," Cindy said. All in all, Bonnie is a nice sort of ghost, generally trying her best to help out.

"She never throws anything," Cindy said.

## Tale End: An Uneasy Feeling

*Located about thirty-five miles northeast of Unalakleet in the Nulato Hills is a shack known as Old Woman Cabin. It was originally established as an Army Signal Corps station in 1903. Later abandoned, it was eventually used as a stopover during the Iditarod Trail Sled Dog Race. It was then dropped for a newer cabin nearby.*

*There's probably good reason why some veteran Iditarod mushers didn't like staying at the cabin. Maybe it's the uneasy feeling many got when they stopped there, or the things that went thump in the night. Or maybe it's the objects that moved around unexplainably.*

*According to one musher, "You'd better be pretty darn tired when you stop so you won't give a hoot about what's going on around you!"*

*Mushers who have stayed there seem to be in a hurry to leave. Some mushers prefer a cold night out on the trail to staying at the cabin.*

*Some say they can't quite put their finger on it, but it's a feeling of evil. What may have happened at Old Woman Cabin is anyone's guess, but whatever it was sure has folks scared.*

THE BLONDE WOMAN IN THE PAINTING HAD BEEN SEEN MANY TIMES. WITNESSES HAVE OBSERVED HER WALKING DOWN THE HALL, THEN SIMPLY VANISHING FROM SIGHT.

# The Specter in Room 321

IF YOU'RE WALKING down South Franklin Street some rainy night in Alaska's capital city of Juneau, you might want to check into the Alaskan Hotel for a drink, a hot meal, and perhaps a haunted room.

If you stay long enough, you might experience something that could make your hair stand on end.

Juneau resident Elva Bontrager knows all about the strange happenings at the Alaskan Hotel. So do many other people. Just talk to the old-timers who frequent the historic hotel. What Elva and others have experienced is etched forever in their memories.

The Alaskan Hotel was established in 1913. The three-story hotel with its small rooms has been in continuous operation since then. Elva tells a remarkable story of what happened to her at the Alaskan.

"I stopped in there with a young woman who used to work there as a maid," Elva said. "We stopped at the bar and restaurant. We sat at the counter and talked with the bartender that she used to work with. We were having coffee. I went to the rest room and when I came back. . . I told my friend, Judy, 'That's quite a painting.' "

Elva was referring to a painting she had just seen in the hallway near the ladies' rest room.

Her friend simply said "Yes."

Three weeks later Elva was at the hotel with another acquaintance. When her friend excused herself to go to the rest room, Elva told her to be sure to look at the painting in the hallway.

"When she came back, she said 'There's no painting there.'

" 'Well, there is,' I said."

Elva went to look. She was shocked to discover that there was no painting and that the wall was a different color. The rest room also had changed. Where three weeks earlier the toilet had been operated with an overhead pull-chain, there was now a standard modern toilet.

Elva found her friend Judy and asked her, "Where's that painting?" Her friend said she didn't know anything about it. Elva then went to the bartender at the Alaskan and asked about the painting, but he assured her there was no such thing.

Elva went home, and with colored pencils she drew what she had seen in the painting. Her drawing showed two young women.

"The one that I remember really well had curly dark hair, and she was wearing a hat pulled over her face a little bit, with either ribbon or red feathers. She had a scar on her upper lip. . . .

"The woman beside her was standing behind a high table, with what I remember in my mind, I called a pot of roses. . . . Her gown was pale, but darker than cream, but yellowish. What I remembered about her, she had blonde hair piled up on top of her head and she was not as good looking as the other one; she had a long face and was very blonde."

Elva showed her drawing to Judy, who seemed quite uncomfortable as she studied it.

"I think it's time to put that away and just forget about it," Judy told Elva.

"Why?" Elva asked.

"I can't tell you how often I've heard that woman described," Judy responded.

It turned out that the blonde woman in the disappearing painting had been seen many times, usually in room 321. She is described as tall and blonde, with a long face. Witnesses have also seen her walking down the hall and, instead of turning the corner, simply vanishing from sight.

"The end of that story is that for the next couple months I didn't dare go back in for fear whether I would see it," Elva said.

The ghost of the Alaskan Hotel carries a tragic story. In life, she was once the bride of a gold prospector. The man told her he was going to the Haines area to search for gold. He put her up at the Alaskan Hotel and said he would return in three weeks.

When her husband failed to return, the woman became desperate. She was out of money and had nowhere to turn. An acquaintance told her there was a way she could support herself, and so she turned to prostitution.

About three months later, the miner returned. When he found out that his wife had been working as a prostitute, he killed her at the hotel.

"Judy said that room 321 cannot be kept clean," Elva stated. "You can go in there and dust and have it nice and when you go back in, it's dusty and things are in disarray."

## An Eskimo Village: How to Deal with Ghosts

ALASKAN ESKIMOS have historically experienced encounters with supernatural beings—spirits that were both respected and feared. They might take on various forms.

Some Eskimos called up spirits by sitting in the dark and talking with their heads bowed and faces covered. The spirits would come with a noise like a great bird. One man who raised his head to see them described a man with bloodless cheeks—a "bad man, dead," recognized as a ghost.

Some of these spirits were as large as a man, some were dwarfish, some appeared as a fleshless skeleton. They made grimaces with gaping, staring eyes and hands outstretched like claws.

People generally had a great dread of these ghosts and were very careful when they were out after dark. One member of each party traveling at night would usually carry a drawn knife, ready for defense against the ghosts.

The knife was also carried to protect against the aurora, the swirling northern lights. Some people feared that the aurora, when it was especially bright, could kill a person by striking him in the back of the neck.

A house in one Eskimo village had a clever contrivance for frightening away ghosts. The man who lived there had secured a cord to the wall with a large knife; the dangling cord had a handle. If the ghost tried to get in the house, it would grab hold of the handle to help itself get inside—thus pulling the knife down upon its head.

At other villages, bits of tobacco were thrown into cemeteries as gifts to placate the ghosts.

In 1883 a U.S. Army officer, identified as Lieutenant P.H. Ray, saw villagers at Point Barrow expelling a ghost. In his report, Ray said he saw women standing at the door of a house, armed with knives and clubs. They swung the weapons over the entrance as people inside the house worked to drive the ghost outside.

Ray said he entered one house and found a woman vigorously driving a ghost out of every corner with a knife. He said that about ten people came forward to speak of injuries they had received from the ghost, which also had been blamed for causing bad weather.

Natives told him the next day that they had succeeded in either killing the ghost or driving it far away.

## Tale End: A Ghostly Visitation

*Imagine yourself in a log cabin up a lonely gulch in the Klondike goldfields. You're sitting there one evening when suddenly the image of a long-dead miner appears—and the old-timer begins talking to you.*

*This is just what happened to gold miner R.A. Fox in 1916, while he was at his cabin on Quartz Creek in the Yukon, about forty miles east of Dawson. Fox knew that a gold miner had been killed years before in an accident in the area. Then the dead miner began appearing to Fox.*

*The apparition materialized now and again. As he sat in a corner of the cabin, the phantom would operate a rocker box, the equipment used for separating gold from gravel, and speak with Fox. After visiting for a while, the old miner would vanish. But he seemed to need this connection with the material world, because he kept reappearing from time to time, one miner speaking to another.*

NOW LATE AT NIGHT, WITH THE DAY'S WORK DONE,

I WATCHED AS LOW CLOUDS HOVERED AROUND

THE MINE STRUCTURES, CREATING AN EERIE EFFECT.

# The Independence Mine:
# A Phantom and His Dog

A LIGHT JULY RAIN fell as low clouds moved in across the Talkeetna
Mountains. It was near midnight, and I saw not a soul down at the
old gold mine, where hikers and other visitors had come during the
day to spend time at the Independence Mine State Historical Park.
The year was 1984, and I was alone at the former mine, carrying out
my job as twenty-four-hour-a-day caretaker of the area while a movie
was being filmed there.

The filmmakers had provided me a motor home to live in, and I loaded it up with sandwiches, cookies, and soda pop from the ski lodge down the hill. A makeshift wooden gate had been put across the road to the mine in order to keep people out at night. My only visitors were parka squirrels, who quickly became my friends after I threw handouts their way. By the end of my two-week stay, I had them sitting in the palm of my hand.

The motor home was parked near the old mine tunnel and the rotting buildings from which the sounds of industry once echoed across the valley. Now the only sound was the splashing of water from the nearby creek. The air was cool that night, and I felt a chill as the rain fell harder.

I thought back on my day's work on the movie set. It was a pleasant experience working on a professional film, and I figured I had the best job in the world. A single scene was shot over and over. In the scene, a young boy tried to walk past a German shepherd, which snarled menacingly—following the orders of its trainer. The boy yelled at the dog to get away.

The director wasn't happy with the performance.

"Cut!" he yelled.

The cameraman focused in again on the scene, ready for the next take as the clapper board slammed down.

"Take two!"

After the scene with the dog was completed, I was instructed to help the special-effects man create some smoke, which was supposed to billow out of a cabin that had been built for the movie—a new cabin that was designed to look old.

We soaked some rubber hosing in dirty oil and placed it in a metal pan that was hung inside the cabin's stovepipe. Through a walkie-talkie, we were given the signal that it was just about time for us to set fire to the oil-soaked hose to create the smoke.

"Three, two, one—roll."

The smoke rose out of the cabin right on cue, making it look like someone had built a fire in the woodstove.

Now late at night, with the day's work done, I watched as low clouds hovered around the mine structures, creating an eerie effect. I looked down over the silent mine, enjoying the solitude.

Then near the bunkhouse, down the hill about two hundred yards away, I saw a lone, dark figure with a dog, moving between two buildings. Man and dog walked across an open area, then vanished.

I walked down to the buildings, but I found nothing. I hid behind one building and peeked out now and then to see if I could spot the elusive visitor. After half an hour I headed back up to camp.

The next day I told people about my visitor. I talked with employees of the historical park and to folks down at the lodge. From them I learned about Phil Coleman and his dog. I was not the first to see them.

Coleman had been foreman of the Independence Mine, and he later worked there as caretaker. He died one evening in the late 1960s as he sat at the bar down at the lodge, having a drink. But his spirit still wanders the mine, I was told. He is joined in his haunts by his dog Sniffer.

I spoke with Ben Wattum, another former caretaker at the mine. Wattum told me that the ghost of Coleman has been known to get into rooms that are locked, and that sometimes the phantom leaves doors ajar.

"I thought I was the only one up here," I said to a state park worker.

"You are," he told me.

The only one still alive, that is.

## Candle Creek: Guidance from the Spirit World

GOLD WAS DISCOVERED on Candle Creek on the Seward Peninsula

in 1901. G.W. Blankenship reported the discovery in that year—along with an eerie story.

Blankenship started from Nome in the summer of 1901, heading for Kotzebue Sound. He loaded his supplies into a small boat, and without a partner hoisted sail for the dangerous voyage up through Bering Strait and along the Arctic coastline.

Once through Bering Strait, Blankenship was blown out to sea by a furious gale. For several days he drifted among the great blocks of ice floating in the water. At this time of great peril, he witnessed a ghost at the stern of the boat, guiding his vessel through the ice. Without this specter, Blankenship said, he would never have made it to shore.

Blankenship said the ghost would motion to him with its hands, showing the direction Blankenship was to steer while he pulled at the oars. He recognized the spirit as that of his deceased father-in-law.

This unearthly assistance didn't end after Blankenship arrived safely on land. The specter also directed Blankenship to gold. Following the directions of the ghost, Blankenship lost no time in traveling up the Kewalik River to Candle Creek. There he established a number of valuable claims, thanks to guidance from the spirit world.

## Tale End: Devil's Country

*Around 1750, a native village along Southeast Alaska's Thomas Bay was buried by a landslide from a steep mountainside. More than five hundred people perished, and from that day, the body of water northeast of Petersburg was known as the Bay of Death.*

*Beginning about 1900, gold-seekers began to enter the Bay of Death and travel up the Patterson River, back into the glacier region. Some of them never returned. The Baird Glacier sits above Thomas Bay, a huge and silent witness to those who have come and gone in the search for the gold said to be waiting in the ridges above the river.*

*Survivors returned with accounts of devil creatures that attacked them. These prospectors sometimes seemed temporarily insane. The creatures were described as standing about four feet high, with clawlike fingers and a body covered with coarse hair. They looked like neither man nor monkey. Oozing sores on their bodies gave off a foul odor.*

*To the people who encountered them, these creatures were truly devils, and thus the area earned the name Devil's Country.*

MY DOG WOULD COME TEARING DOWN THE
STAIRS AND LEAP OVER THE COUCH, AND WHINE
AND WHIMPER AND SHAKE. ONE WONDERS WHAT SHE
MIGHT HAVE SEEN AND COULDN'T TELL US ABOUT.

# The Haunted Cabin

THE OLD TALKEETNA cabin has become known for the strange
sightings and other incidents that happen there. Families who have
lived in the two-story log cabin tell of apparitions, of having a bed
picked up and shaken, of lights spontaneously switching on and off—
all the typical activities of ghostly beings that want to let you know
they are there.

Kim Follet and her family lived in the roomy cabin for four years,
beginning in October 1991.

"It was an interesting house. We found old money hidden in the wall. It had been stashed many years before. It was just dollar bills."

The place "was creepy, but I knew it couldn't hurt me," she said.

"At night when you went to bed there were curtains that were hooked open. They had loops around the sides of the curtains to keep them open. When I'd get up in the morning, those would all be closed."

Then there were the people who weren't there.

"You could hear people walking upstairs. I know they weren't there, but you could hear them. Everybody would be downstairs, so we knew it wasn't one of us. . . . If you were upstairs, you could hear them downstairs, and if you were downstairs, you could hear them upstairs. It sounded like someone with real heavy boots stomping around."

The family dog knew something was wrong.

"My dog would come tearing down the stairs and leap over the couch, and whine and whimper in the middle of the floor and shake. She didn't like it very much. One wonders what she might have seen and couldn't tell us about.

"My dog would never go down into the basement. She'd bark and growl if the door was open."

The cat was another matter: "The cat loved that basement. It was crying to go down in the basement and I wouldn't let it. The doorknob turned while I was looking at it and the door opened and the cat ran on down. I was pretty horrified!"

Kim avoided the basement herself.

"There was a propane burner in the basement that I'd have to turn back on periodically. We'd run out of propane and I'd have to go down and light it. I got so I'd just take a lantern with me, because the lights would flicker off when I got down to the bottom of the stairs. It would be pitch black. I hated that basement! It was like they were waiting for me.

"I didn't see anything, I heard it. My son said he got hit with a jelly bean in the back. He was pretty upset about it."

"There was a rumor that a kid got killed by a grizzly years ago in the backyard. I don't know if that's true or not. Our little girl was four years old when we first moved there. There was a swing set out back, and every time she'd get near it, she'd hear a sucking-type sound. She wouldn't go over there."

Kim recalls a frequent incident in the simple task of pulling a chair away from the dining room table: it would feel heavy, like someone was sitting in it. Occasionally a room would feel especially cold, "as if a presence were there." And when she was in the shower, "the lights would flicker on and off. My husband would holler like one of us was doing it." Not so.

"When things started first happening, I thought it was haunted right off. I got the creeps right away. . . . We endured there for four years because there wasn't any other place to move to. It was creepy but we just lived with it. I didn't feel threatened. Nothing harmful ever happened. It was just spooky."

Kim says she is not the only occupant of the cabin who has come face to face with the supernatural. A fellow who used to cut wood for Kim told her about the girls from outlying areas who used to lodge at the cabin during the school year. He said the girls had stories about strange happenings at the cabin—such as the stove turning on by itself.

A friend of Kim's who once lived in the cabin also sensed an unearthly presence. She felt a disembodied hand touch her in the back as she stood at the top of the basement stairs. And she once saw the reflection in a window of a lumberjack—just the reflection, with no one causing it.

Kim finally had "a little talk" with the ghosts of her cabin, telling them: "You know, I have to live here, and I'd rather not see you or hear you."

## Grayling: The Forbidden Island

THE SMALL TOWN OF Grayling, Alaska, is situated on the Yukon River, twenty-two miles above Anvik. For more than a century, residents of this quiet town have watched the river glide by.

The Yukon is a lifeline for Grayling and other river communities. On a summer day, you'll see boats coming and going, with some people fishing for salmon and others hunting game along the shores and on river islands. Barges arrive in summer, carrying supplies for the town.

The river villages also have their old cemeteries, where generation after generation of residents are buried. Some of the graveyards can no longer be seen; they have been left to grow over, reclaimed by nature. Every once in a while, the people here are forcibly reminded of the past as they step where perhaps they are not wanted.

Max Embree, a missionary with Interact Missions of Alaska, recalls the day he and an Athabascan friend went hunting. They traveled in a boat powered by an outboard motor. His friend saw a large moose on an island downstream from Grayling, and they went in pursuit.

Cutting the motor, they glided onto the island's muddy beach, which was fringed with tall grass and shrouded in alders. A few spruce trees leaned out over the river, where high water had eroded their roots. The men left the boat and, carrying their rifles, started to make their way through the brush toward the moose. Suddenly they both felt terribly ill. They thought it might be the flu, and they decided to return to Grayling.

Back in the boat, only halfway across the river, the illness disappeared. They were both feeling well. So they returned to the island and resumed the hunt. They immediately felt ill again, and they decided once more to leave. Embree was too sick to talk, and his friend was also in bad shape. But as soon as they were away from the island, the illness again left them.

The odd events puzzled them no end. They related their story to village elders, who may have given them the answer they needed. They were told that the island was the site of an ancient Indian burial place. They had accidentally stumbled onto forbidden ground.


## Tale End: The Schoolhouse at Kiana

*About sixty miles east of Kotzebue in northwest Alaska is the village of Kiana, situated along the Kobuk River near the foot of the Baird Mountains. You can get there by air, dog team, or boat.*

*The wooden schoolhouse in Kiana has been around since the 1930s. Some of the old-timers in the area used to attend classes there and have many good memories of the little school that included grades one through twelve.*

*A teacher at the school in the early 1950s, Mr. Hall, is remembered by many former students. He would walk along the rows of desks, helping his students, aided by the crutches he used after a bout with polio.*

*Mr. Hall and his wife were noted for putting on great Halloween parties for the children. He always dressed in costume, and he would thump down the hallway and with a deep voice say, "Who's got my tail?"*

*This teacher then grew ill. He was flown out of Kiana to a hospital, where he died.*

*Since then, some people in Kiana have seen signs that perhaps Mr. Hall didn't really want to leave the village. They say the sound of his crutches thumping on the wooden floor can still be heard from time to time at the Kiana schoolhouse.*

RED COONEY SAID HE FELT THERE WAS
NOTHING TO FEAR—AS LONG AS OTHER FOLKS
WERE AROUND. BUT WHEN HE WAS ALONE,
IT WAS A DIFFERENT STORY.

# Voices from Another Dimension

A COLD BREEZE BLOWS from the north, off the Alaska Range. Far in
the valley below, the icy Maclaren River snakes its way from this range
and pours into the Big Susitna River, whose waters eventually end up
in Knik Arm and the Gulf of Alaska. If it's a clear day, the high peaks
of Mount Hays, Mount Hess, and Mount Deborah can be seen
looming up to the north.

The Maclaren River region has offered up gold and copper to
prospectors. Caribou and grizzlies roam the rolling, often treeless

landscape, where moss and alders carpet buried rocks and glacial debris from the past ice age. The area is also known for its fishing and for its fish tales.

There are days out on the moss-covered hills when, if you listen carefully, you might hear voices. Or is it just the wind, or the gurgling of water flowing over the rocks?

Trappers, miners, and dog team drivers once wrested a living from this region, and sometimes left legends after their passing. There's the story of Ben French, a trapper and prospector who had a cabin on the Maclaren River just below Round Mountain and another cabin on the Middle Fork, five miles above its confluence with the main fork.

French would fish for salmon and dry them for his winter food; then he would head to Meiers Roadhouse and Gulkana to sell his furs and pick up supplies for the coming year. It was rumored that French had a gold mine on the headwaters of the Maclaren. He always brought out some gold to trade, but he never revealed where he got it.

In 1928, Ben French made his last trip to the roadhouse. On his return to the Maclaren River, he was caught in a snowstorm and apparently died. Somewhere near Dickey Lake, a search party discovered French's sled, but his body was never found. There are those who still wonder if a lucrative gold mine awaits some fortunate prospector, up on the headwaters of the Maclaren.

After the Denali Highway came through in the 1950s, this region was opened up to auto travel. No more would the adventurer have to struggle along tundra trails on sleds drawn by horses or dogs. Only remnants of trails once hacked out by hopeful prospectors can be seen today.

From the Richardson Highway, starting at Paxson Lodge, the Denali Highway stretches out nearly 150 miles, ending at Cantwell along the Parks Highway. Denali Highway is actually a rough gravel road, with plenty of places to stop. One of the more notable landmarks along the way is the Maclaren River Lodge, at Mile 41.

The lodge was built in the 1950s by Whitey Mathison, an old-timer from Fairbanks. It was eventually taken over by Red Cooney, who came to Alaska in the 1960s from Minnesota to work in the oil industry. Looking for a diversion, he purchased the lodge in 1971.

When Red bought the lodge, Whitey was living in an old cabin on the site, a place constructed of logs, pallets, and other wood pieces, enough to build a weatherproof shelter. Whitey Mathison continued to live in the cabin until he died, a couple of years after Red bought the place.

About that time, Red quit his oil-industry job on the North Slope and moved to the lodge to run it personally. With Whitey now gone, Red Cooney and a friend decided to stay in his old cabin—and that's when strange incidents began to occur.

"I would wake up at night in the cabin and hear women's voices talking," Red says. "It always sounded like two women talking. You could never understand what they were saying, but it was two women having a conversation.

"I thought it must be the river. I'd lay there and listen, and think it's got to be the nearby Maclaren River, rippling or something.

"I'd hear this night after night. One morning I got up and I said to my friend, 'Did you hear the women talking?'

"He said, 'Did you hear that too?'"

A friend of Red's known as Little Pete, along with his girlfriend, came to the lodge that summer. The couple worked there, and they also reported some odd goings-on—including the disembodied voices of two women talking and an actual sighting of the pair.

"Little Pete's girlfriend happened to look out the kitchen window and saw two women walking across the yard near the lodge," Red said. "She's the only one in all the years at the lodge who has actually seen them.

"She went out of the kitchen and over to the big heavy lodge door to let them in. Well, there wasn't anybody there."

Red's sister Mary is the only person who has ever been able to understand anything of what the women are saying. Red hadn't told Mary about the voices. In fact, he didn't tell a lot of people, for fear of being laughed at.

One morning, Mary told Red there were two women talking outside her window the previous night.

"I said, 'There were? What did they say?'

"She said one was telling the other, 'This is my room.'"

For other people, "the voices were always a murmur," Red said. "You could tell it was two women's voices, but always a murmur."

No one knows who these women are. There seems to be no history behind the voices, no women whose deaths might have led to their reappearance as talking spirits.

The stories about the talking women go on and on. A man who had spent a night near the lodge in his motor home came into the lodge in the morning, saying:

"Man, I didn't get any sleep last night."

"Why not?" he was asked.

"There were women talking around my camper all night!"

A fellow who was helping remodel rooms at the lodge paused before entering one room, because he heard women's voices. He left to ask if the room had been rented, and he was told that it had not. When he checked the room, of course no one was there.

Red Cooney said he felt there was nothing to fear—as long as other folks were around. But when he was alone, it was a different story.

"I wouldn't sleep in the back room by myself," he said. "I'd wake up and be looking at the wall and I'd know there was something looking at my back. There was always that feeling someone was there if you were by yourself."

The talking women were the biggest unseen presence at the lodge, but there seemed to be some others. Because sometimes lights would go off by themselves; tools would disappear; odd footsteps could be heard. Red figured there was at least one other ghost at the place.

Red later sold the lodge and returned to work on the North Slope. But one late fall, he arranged to stay for a while at Whitey's old cabin. The new owners had already left the lodge for the winter.

It was a cool, crisp day as Red drove to the lodge. There was frost in the morning, and the hillsides had turned brown and gold. The Alaska Range had its familiar fresh coating of snow, and winter was indeed knocking on the door.

"I wanted to spend some time by myself," Red recalls. "As I drove up the highway from Paxson, I thought about the ghost. I thought, *I hope the ghost doesn't bother me.*"

"I went up there, went in the cabin, got everything ready. Suddenly I heard something walking on the porch.

"I took a couple steps toward the windows to look out, and then it was like somebody took a pitchfork or a rake and scratched the whole length of the cabin. And that's the only time it really scared me, bad.

"It was a real hard scratch down the wall, pretty fast, in two or three steps. It got right next to me and then it was just like an explosion! My heart was up in my throat!

"The explosion was as if someone shot a gun there. Then I managed to calm myself down. *Ghosts don't hurt you,* I reminded myself. *Calm down. Calm down.* I calmed right down.

"I made up my mind the ghosts aren't going to bother me."

Red went hunting, then came back and had supper. He laid in his bed and read a book and never felt more comfortable in his life.

"Here's my theory. The ghosts thought everyone had left for the winter, and they settled in. Then I showed up again. They were pissed!"

Red also tells of the time he was at the lodge with a few of his relatives and other people, getting the place ready to open up for the new season. One of the women walked down the hallway to take a shower, and Red's nephew Jimmie saw her enter the bathroom.

A little while later the same woman walked in the front door. Jimmie was a bit puzzled, but he didn't say anything. This woman then walked down the hall to take a shower, but stopped because the room was in use.

She asked Jimmie if he knew who was in the shower room.

Jimmie said he thought *she* was.

When they opened the door, they found no one.

That same day, Red was looking for two of the women who were at the lodge.

"I heard them talking, and I went to the back of the lodge and I'm calling them. They didn't answer. I went back out and couldn't find them. I looked out and they're both out at the airplane, about one hundred yards away!"

Red then realized it was his ghosts again, the phantom talking women of the Maclaren.

## Tale End: The Woman in White

*She can be seen wandering among the tombstones on certain nights. Her long, white dress flutters behind her as she walks along the hillside.*

*Located on a lush, green slope on the outskirts of Fairbanks is Birch Hill Cemetery, with its graves both old and new. The famous and the near-famous are among those who occupy Birch Hill.*

*One of these is Al Mayo, one of the more colorful sourdoughs who came to the Yukon Territory in the 1880s and operated trading posts along the Yukon River watershed of Alaska and Canada.*

*His neighbors include Aaron Van Curler, a gold miner in the Upper Chena River for many years, a man who looked much like Abraham Lincoln.*

*Ben Falls is also buried at Birch Hill, along with Jay Livengood and Teddy Hudson. These three played big roles in the gold-rush history of Livengood, a mining community about seventy miles north of Fairbanks.*

*The most visible resident of Birch Hill is the young woman whose spirit walks among the gravestones. She is sighted now and then by graveyard visitors, mostly in the twilight hours. She often wears a flowing white dress characteristic of the early 1900s.*

*No one knows who she is, and no one has seen her face. She is one of many whose restless spirit wanders the Far North.*

# Sources

The author thanks and acknowledges
the following sources for the stories in this book.

No Time to Mess with A Ghost
  Jean Ashby Huddleston
  Walter Phillips

Knik: Voices in the Woods
  Linda Dahl

An Eternal Vigil
  Lauri Rapuzzi
  Golden North Hotel

A Restless Night in Nenana
  Rick Rapuzzi
  *Alaska,* by Merle F. Colby (1940)

The Ladue House: Footsteps on the Stairs
  Nancy Schmidt

A Place of Sadness
  Sam Holloway

'We Got Ghosts'
  Rick Shields
  Roberta Sheldon
  Matanuska-Susitna Borough
    History Office

Deadman's Camp: A Friendly Spirit
  Lynette Clark

Haunting the Bureaucracy
  Mike Marsh

An Air of Mystery
  Susan Knapman
  Mike Holland
  U.S. Geological Survey
  Circle Mining District Museum;
    Central, Alaska

The Disappearing Woman
  Mike Carpenter

Murder Most Foul
  *Anchorage Daily Times* (1939)
  *The Mystery of the Cache Creek Murders,*
    by Roberta Sheldon (2001)

The Phantom Cat Train
  Red Cooney

The Model T
  Jimmy Scott

The Hairy Man of Iliamna
  Fred Dyson

The Sinrock Hills: Ghost Herder
  *Nome Nugget* (1901)
  Clarence Towarok

The White House
  John Tronrud

The Spirited Brothel
  Lauri Rapuzzi

Baranof Castle: A Tragic
    Love Affair
  Orrine Denslow
  Sitka Historical Society
  *History of Alaska,* by Hubert Bancroft
    (1890)
  *Report on Population and Resources of
    Alaska at the Eleventh Census: 1890.*
  U.S. Census Office

The Ship That Vanished
  *Alaska Sportsman* magazine

The Ghost Smoked a Pipe
  Walt Phillips
  Barbara Strang

The Crying of Children
  Howard Ulrich

Apparitions of the Air
  Ingrid Pedersen

The Restless Miner
  Jamie Hall

Nightmare of the Past
  Lael Morgan
  *History of Alaska,* by Hubert Bancroft
    (1890)
  *Report on Population and Resources of
    Alaska at the Eleventh Census: 1890.*
    U.S. Census Office

Wickersham House: The Judge
    Loved Bacon
  Pat Wendt
  Elva Brontrager
  State of Alaska

No Place to Spend a Night
  Walt Phillips

Headless Valley
  *Dawson Daily News* (1911 and 1916)
  *Dangerous River,* by R. M. Patterson
    (1954)
  *Alaska Sportsman* magazine
  Max Embree
  Sam Holloway

The Mendeltna Lodge: Bonnie
    The Friendly Ghost
  Cindy Lockert

An Uneasy Feeling
  Joe Redington

The Specter in Room 321
  Elva Brontrager

An Eskimo Village: How to Deal
    with Ghosts
  Smithsonian Institution Bureau of
    American Ethnology, 9th Annual
    Report (1888)
  "Ethnological Results of the
    Point Barrow Expedition,"
    by John Murdoch (1885)

A Ghostly Visitation
  *Dawson Daily News (1916)*

The Independence Mine: A Phantom
    and His Dog
  Ron Wendt

Candle Creek: Guidance from the
    Spirit World
  *Nome Nugget* (1905)

Devil's Country
  *The Strangest Story Ever Told,* by Harry
    D. Colp (1997)

The Haunted Cabin
  Kim Follet

Grayling: The Forbidden Island
  Max Embree

The Schoolhouse at Kiana
  Lorry Schuerch

Voices from Another Dimension
  Red Cooney

The Woman in White
  Ron Wendt

# About the Author

Ron Wendt was raised on his family's homestead near Fairbanks and his father's mining claims in the Circle gold fields of eastern Alaska. He developed an early interest in Alaska history by exploring ghost towns and mining camps and talking with old-timers from the gold rush era. He has worked as a gold miner, newspaper reporter, photographer, college instructor, construction worker, and maintenance man.

Wendt's articles and photos have appeared in numerous publications, including *Alaska* magazine, *Alaska Geographic, Anchorage Daily News, Rock & Gem* magazine, and *Christian Science Monitor.* He owns Goldstream Publications, of Wasilla, Alaska, which publishes the many books he has written, including *Where to Prospect for Gold in Alaska Without Getting Shot!; Strange, Amazing True Tales of Alaska; Gold, Ghost Towns & Grizzlies;* and *Alaska Dog Mushing Guide.* He also publishes *The Alaska Goldfield* magazine and *Alaska Tales and Trails Magazine.*

---

## ACCIDENTAL ADVENTURER
Memoir of the First Woman to Climb Mount McKinley
Barbara Washburn, paperback, $16.95

## ARCTIC BUSH PILOT:
Memoir by James "Andy" Anderson as told to Jim Rearden
Paperback, $16.95

## BEYOND THE KILLING TREE
Memoir by Stephen Reynolds, hardbound edition, $19.95

## BIRD GIRL & THE MAN WHO FOLLOWED THE SUN
An Athabascan Indian Legend from Alaska
Velma Wallis, hardbound edition, $19.95

## CHEATING DEATH: Amazing Survival Stories from Alaska
Larry Kaniut, paperback, $14.95

## EXPLORING THE UNKNOWN
Historic Diaries of Bradford Washburn's Alaska/Yukon Expeditions
Dr. Bradford Washburn, edited by Lew Freedman
Large format paperback with numerous photos, $19.95

## IDITAROD CLASSICS:
Tales of the Trail Told by the Men & Women Who Race Across Alaska
Lew Freedman, illustrated by Jon Van Zyle, paperback, $12.95

## STRANGE STORIES OF ALASKA & THE YUKON
Ed Ferrell, paperback, $13.95

---

**EPICENTER PRESS**

*Alaska Book Adventures*™

These titles can be found or special-ordered at your local bookstore.
A wide assortment of Alaska books also can be ordered at the publisher's website,
www.EpicenterPress.com, or by calling 1-800-950-6663.